POKÉMON™ X•Y

STORY
Hidenori Xsaka

ART
Satoshi Yamamoto

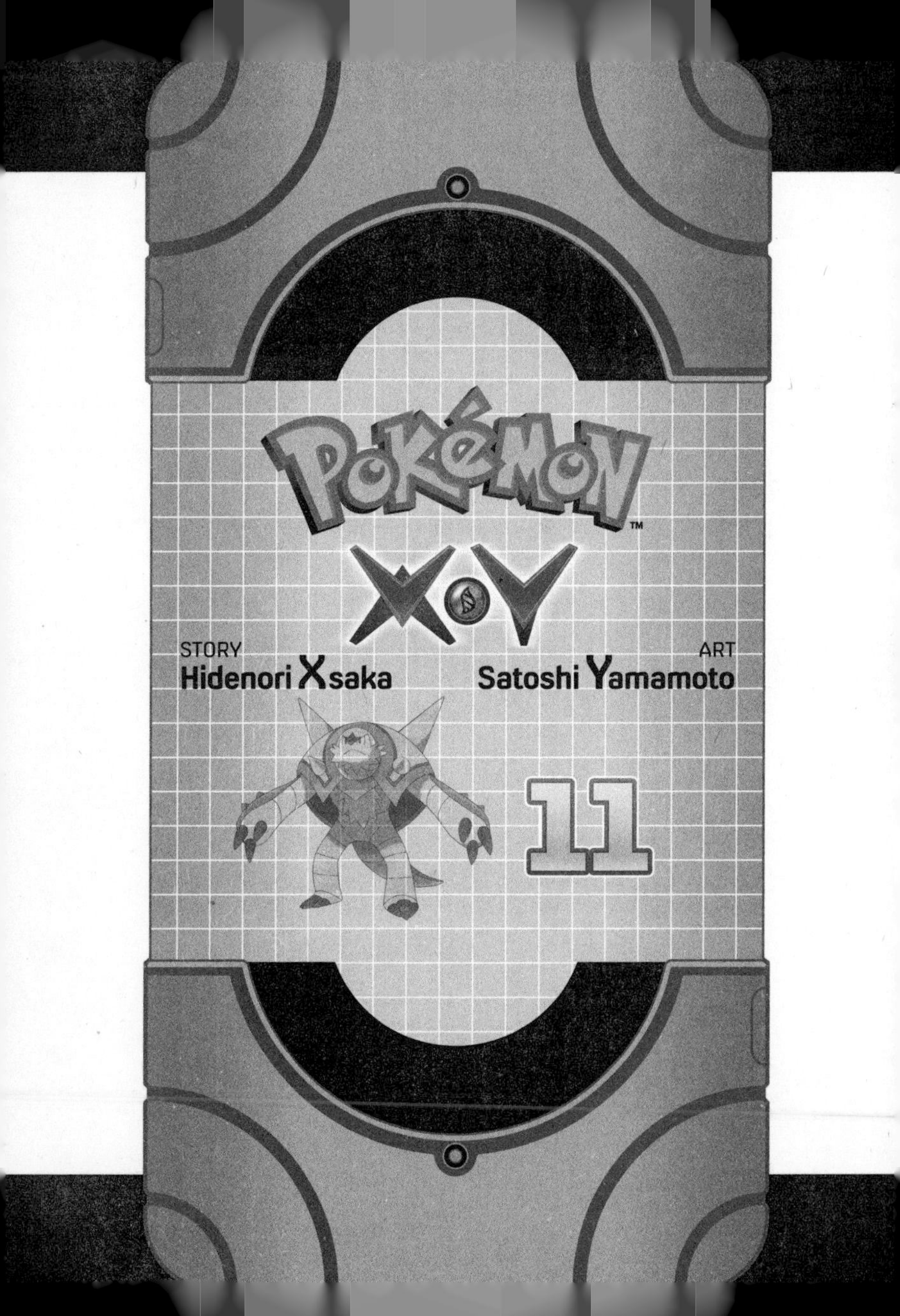

11

CHARACTERS

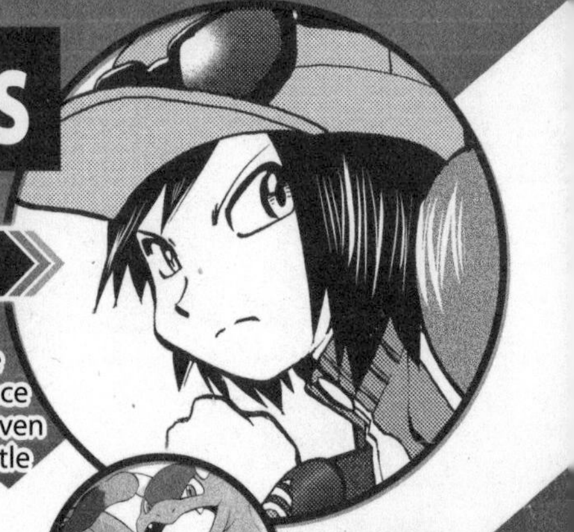

X

The main character of this chapter, and one of five close childhood friends. He was once a highly skilled Trainer who even won the Junior Pokémon Battle Tournament, but now...

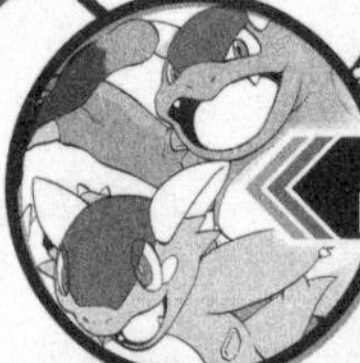

KANGA & LI'L KANGA

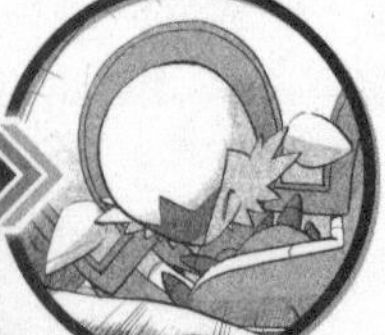

MARISSO

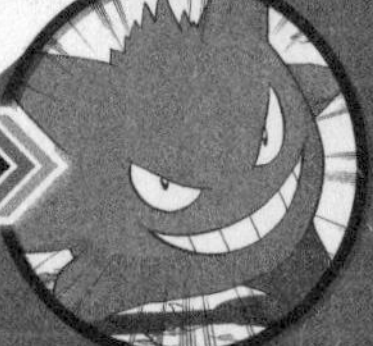

GARMA

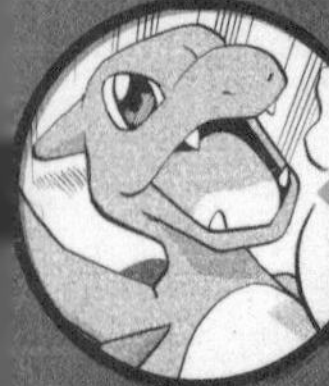

SALAMÈ

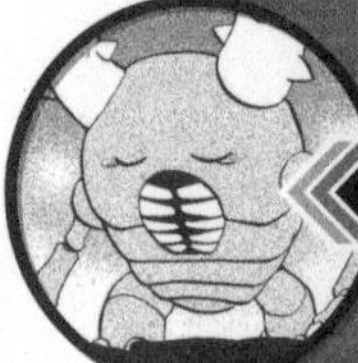

RUTE

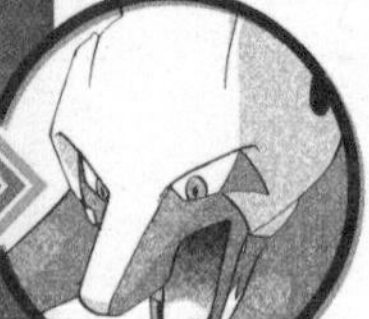

ÉLEC

OUR STORY THUS FAR...

In Vaniville Town in the Kalos region, X is a Pokémon Trainer child prodigy. But then he falls into a depression. A sudden attack by the Legendary Pokémon Xerneas and Yveltal, controlled by Team Flare, forces X out into the world. He and his closest childhood friends—Y, Trevor, Tierno and Shauna—are now on the run.

Y receives a Mega Ring and becomes a Mega Evolution successor. Then X and his friends learn the whereabouts of Team Flare's new hideout and head there for a showdown. But along the way they are ambushed by five scientists from Team Flare...!

MEET THE

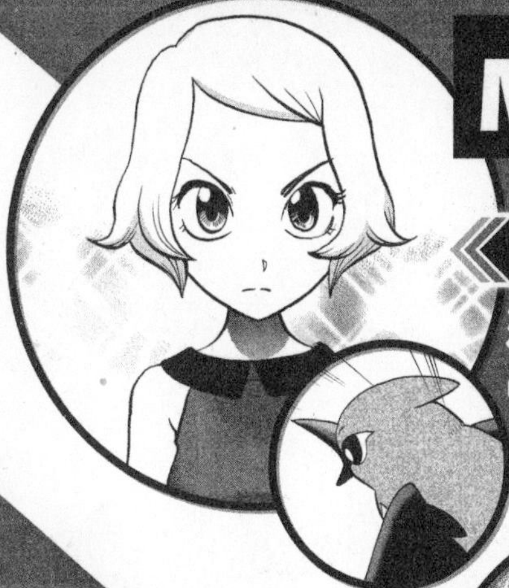

Y

X's best friend, a Sky Trainer trainee. Her full name is Yvonne Gabena.

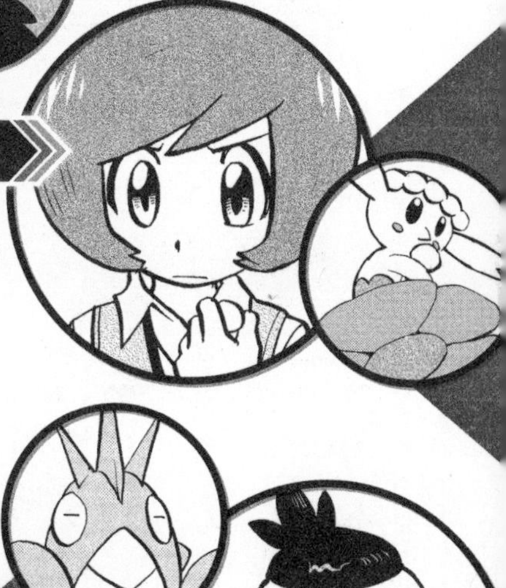

TREVOR

One of the five friends. A quiet boy who hopes to become a fine Pokémon Researcher one day.

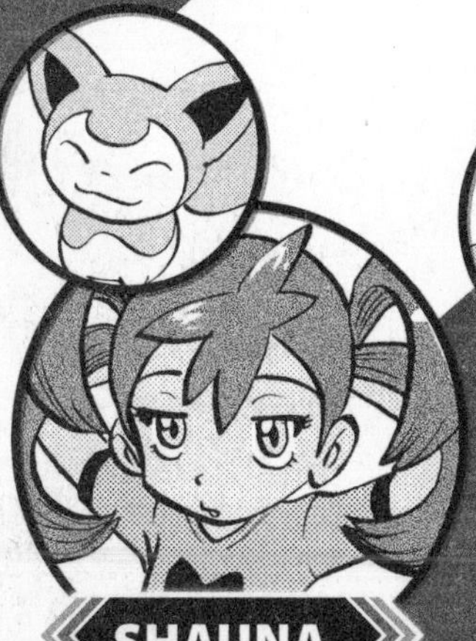

SHAUNA

One of the five friends. Her dream is to become a Furfrou Groomer. She is quick to speak her mind.

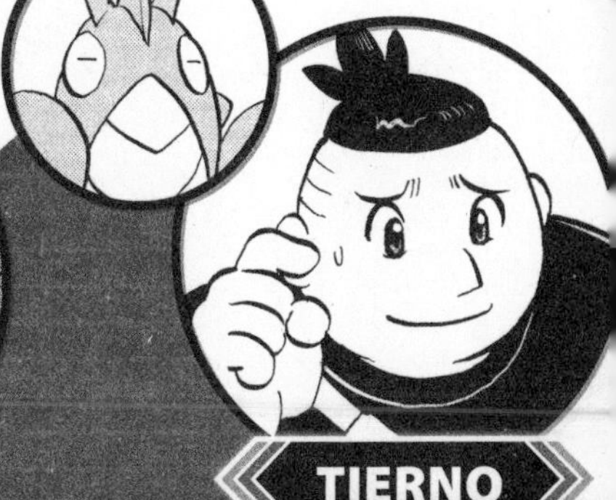

TIERNO

One of the five friends. A bi
boy with an even bigger
heart. He is currently traini
to become a dancer.

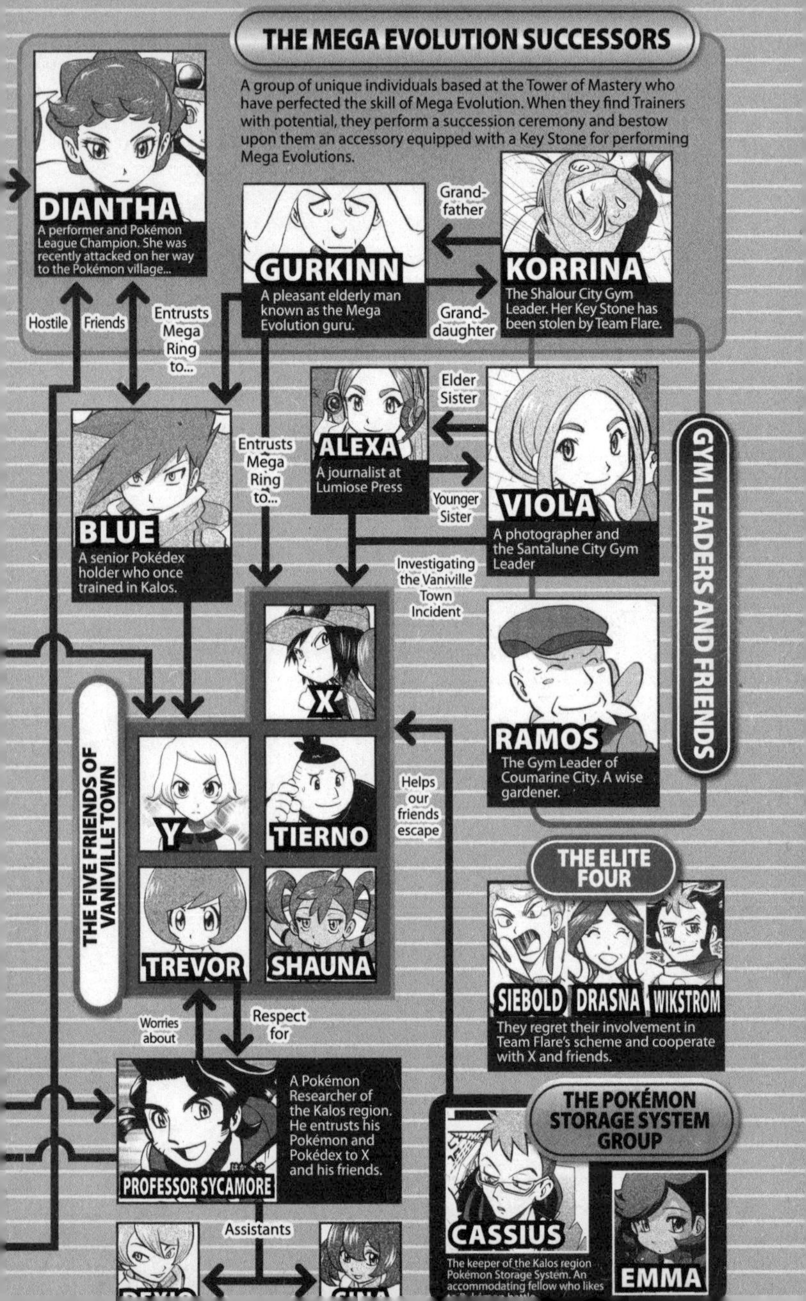
THE MEGA EVOLUTION SUCCESSORS
A group of unique individuals based at the Tower of Mastery who have perfected the skill of Mega Evolution. When they find Trainers with potential, they perform a succession ceremony and bestow upon them an accessory equipped with a Key Stone for performing Mega Evolutions.
DIANTHA
A performer and Pokémon League Champion. She was recently attacked on her way to the Pokémon village...
GURKINN
A pleasant elderly man known as the Mega Evolution guru.
Grand-father
Grand-daughter
KORRINA
The Shalour City Gym Leader. Her Key Stone has been stolen by Team Flare.
Hostile
Friends
Entrusts Mega Ring to...
GYM LEADERS AND FRIENDS
Elder Sister
ALEXA
A journalist at Lumiose Press
Younger Sister
VIOLA
A photographer and the Santalune City Gym Leader
BLUE
A senior Pokédex holder who once trained in Kalos.
Entrusts Mega Ring to...
Investigating the Vaniville Town Incident
X
RAMOS
The Gym Leader of Coumarine City. A wise gardener.
THE FIVE FRIENDS OF VANIVILLE TOWN
Y
TIERNO
Helps our friends escape
TREVOR
SHAUNA
THE ELITE FOUR
SIEBOLD
DRASNA
WIKSTROM
They regret their involvement in Team Flare's scheme and cooperate with X and friends.
Worries about
Respect for
A Pokémon Researcher of the Kalos region. He entrusts his Pokémon and Pokédex to X and his friends.
PROFESSOR SYCAMORE
THE POKÉMON STORAGE SYSTEM GROUP
Assistants
CASSIUS
The keeper of the Kalos region Pokémon Storage System. An accommodating fellow who likes
EMMA

CHARACTER CORRELATION CHART

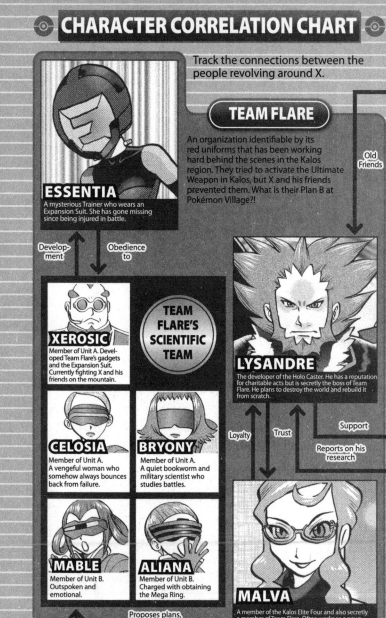

Track the connections between the people revolving around X.

TEAM FLARE

An organization identifiable by its red uniforms that has been working hard behind the scenes in the Kalos region. They tried to activate the Ultimate Weapon in Kalos, but X and his friends prevented them. What is their Plan B at Pokémon Village?!

ESSENTIA
A mysterious Trainer who wears an Expansion Suit. She has gone missing since being injured in battle.

Development

Obedience to

TEAM FLARE'S SCIENTIFIC TEAM

XEROSIC
Member of Unit A. Developed Team Flare's gadgets and the Expansion Suit. Currently fighting X and his friends on the mountain.

CELOSIA
Member of Unit A. A vengeful woman who somehow always bounces back from failure.

BRYONY
Member of Unit A. A quiet bookworm and military scientist who studies battles.

MABLE
Member of Unit B. Outspoken and emotional.

ALIANA
Member of Unit B. Charged with obtaining the Mega Ring.

Proposes plans, assists others

Old Friends

LYSANDRE
The developer of the Holo Caster. He has a reputation for charitable acts but is secretly the boss of Team Flare. He plans to destroy the world and rebuild it from scratch.

Loyalty

Trust

Support

Reports on his research

MALVA
A member of the Kalos Elite Four and also secretly a member of Team Flare. Often works as a news reporter and manipulates the media to the benefit of Team Flare.

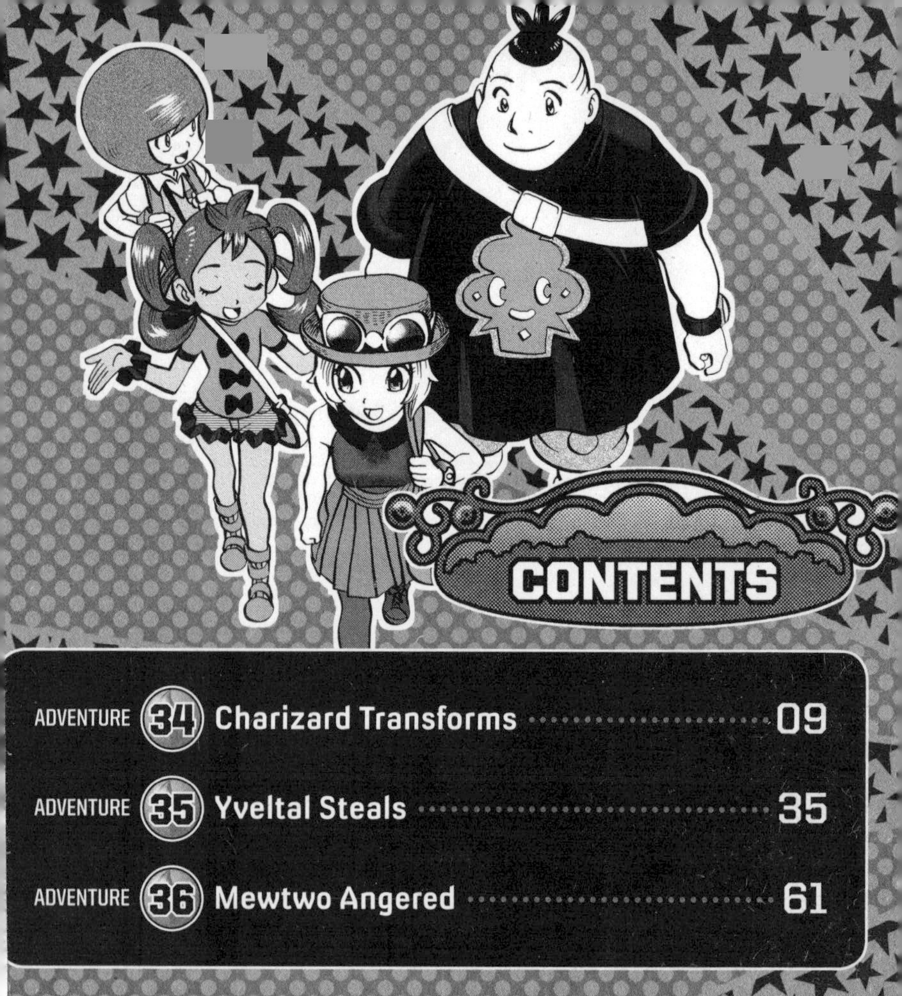

CONTENTS

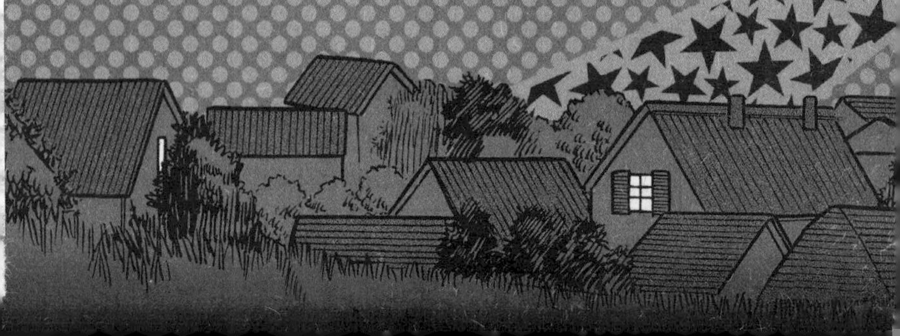

Adventure 34 Charizard Transforms

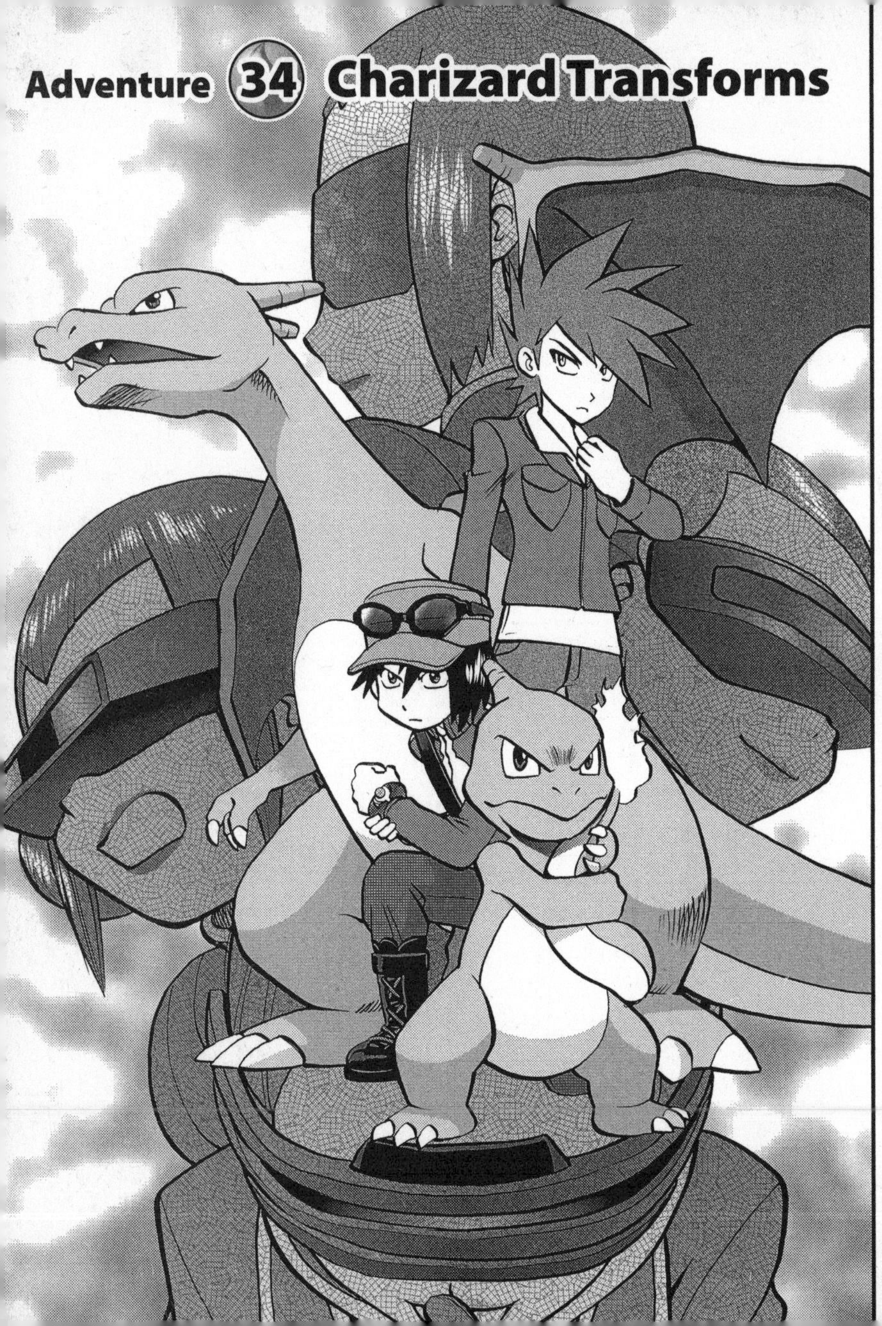

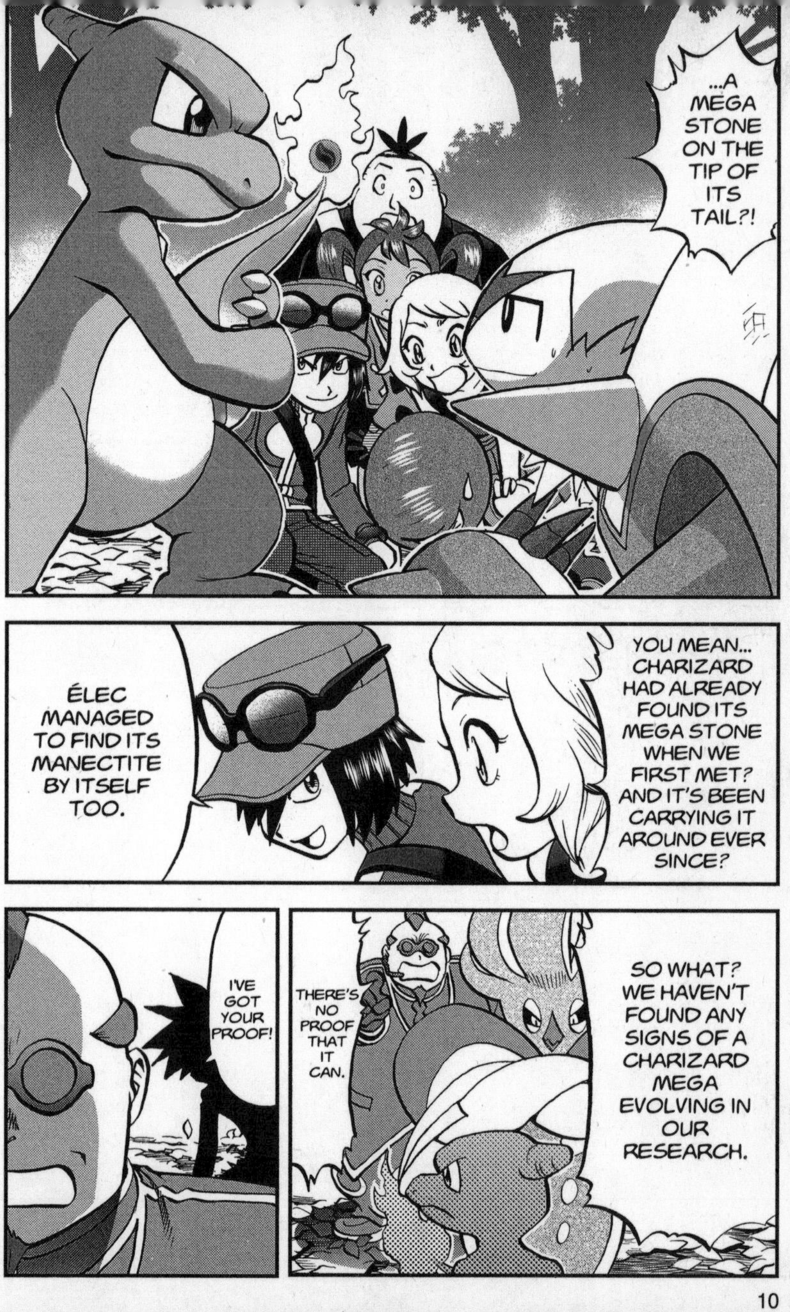
...A MEGA STONE ON THE TIP OF ITS TAIL?!
YOU MEAN... CHARIZARD HAD ALREADY FOUND ITS MEGA STONE WHEN WE FIRST MET? AND IT'S BEEN CARRYING IT AROUND EVER SINCE?
ÉLEC MANAGED TO FIND ITS MANECTITE BY ITSELF TOO.
SO WHAT? WE HAVEN'T FOUND ANY SIGNS OF A CHARIZARD MEGA EVOLVING IN OUR RESEARCH.
THERE'S NO PROOF THAT IT CAN.
I'VE GOT YOUR PROOF!

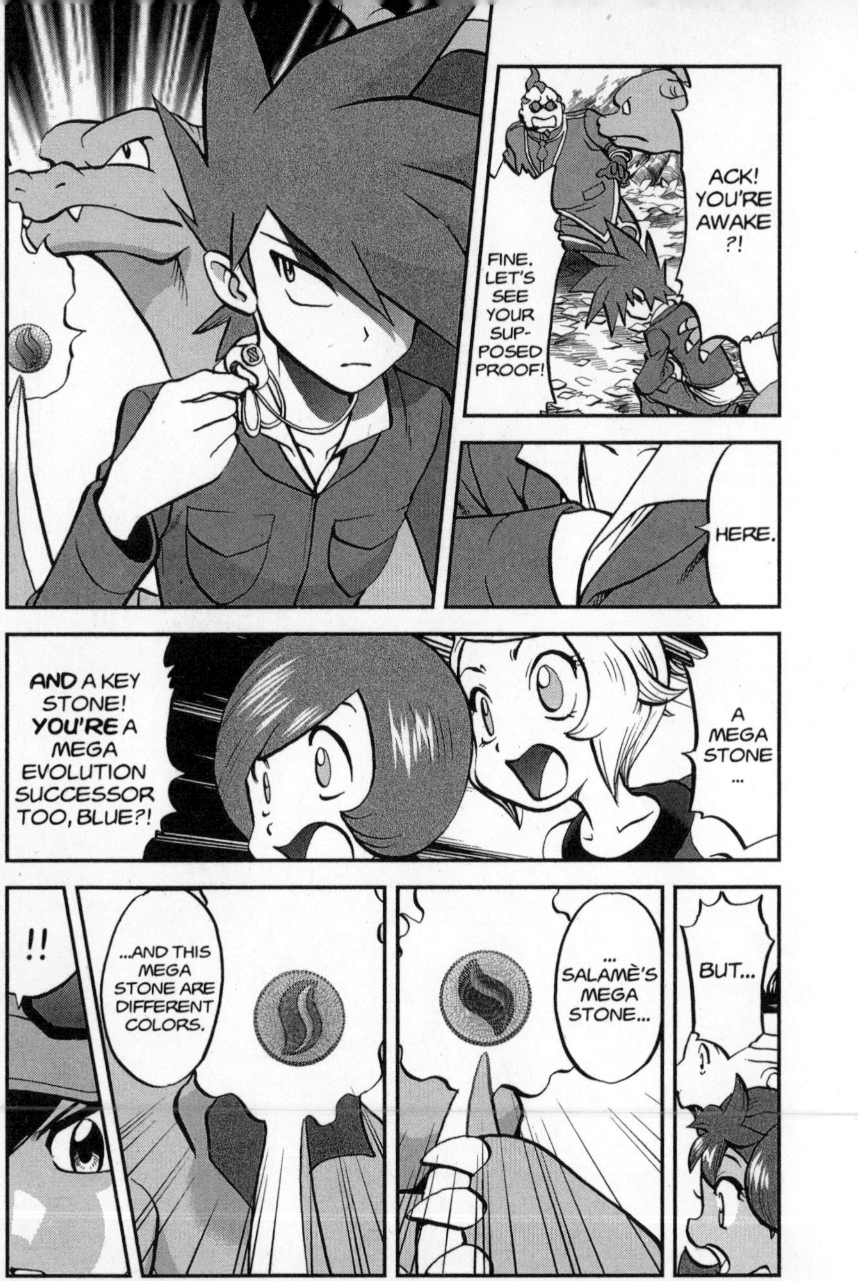
ACK! YOU'RE AWAKE?!
FINE. LET'S SEE YOUR SUP-POSED PROOF!
HERE.
A MEGA STONE...
AND A KEY STONE! YOU'RE A MEGA EVOLUTION SUCCESSOR TOO, BLUE?!
BUT...
... SALAMÈ'S MEGA STONE...
...AND THIS MEGA STONE ARE DIFFERENT COLORS.
!!

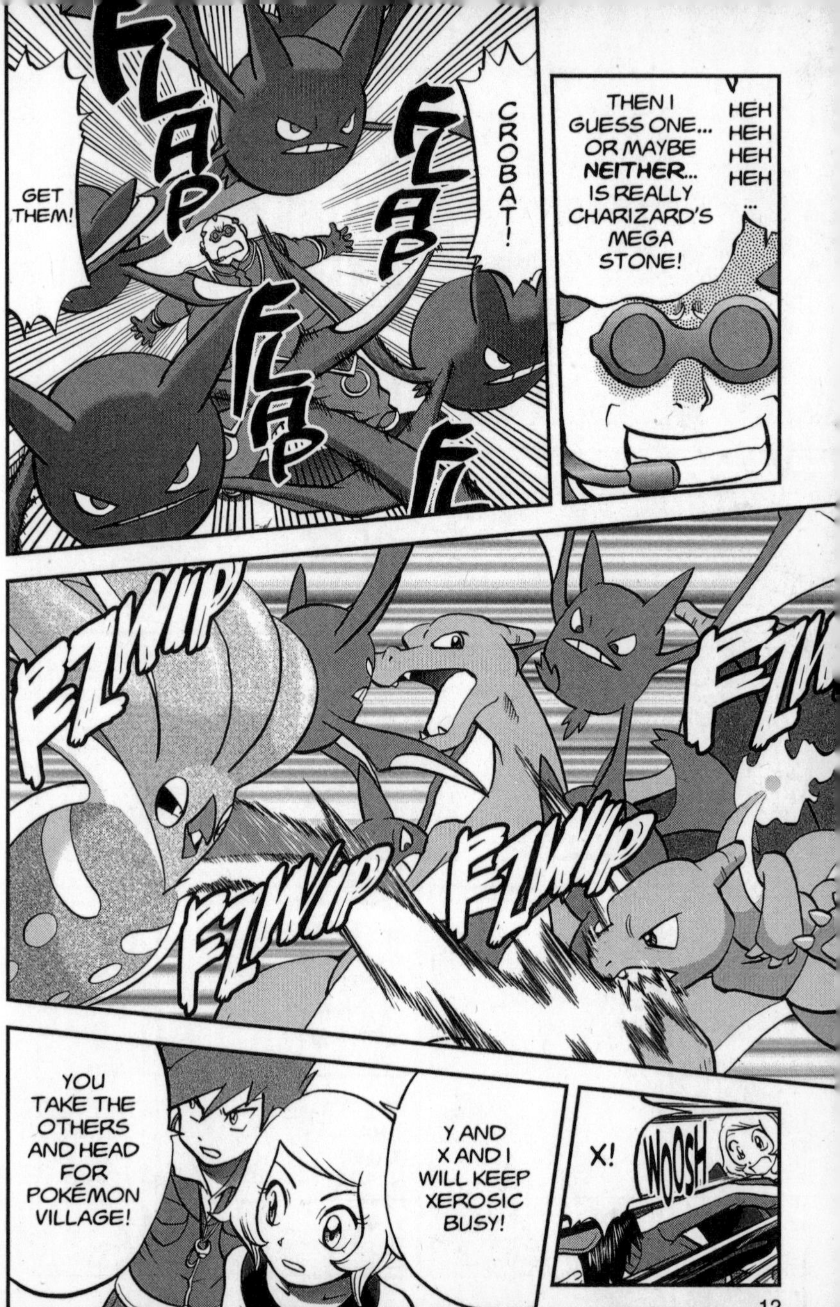
HEH HEH HEH HEH ...
THEN I GUESS ONE... OR MAYBE **NEITHER**... IS REALLY CHARIZARD'S MEGA STONE!
CROBAT!
FLAP
FLAP
FLAP
FL
GET THEM!
FZ
FZWIP
FZWIP
FZWIP
WOOSH
X!
Y AND X AND I WILL KEEP XEROSIC BUSY!
YOU TAKE THE OTHERS AND HEAD FOR POKÉMON VILLAGE!

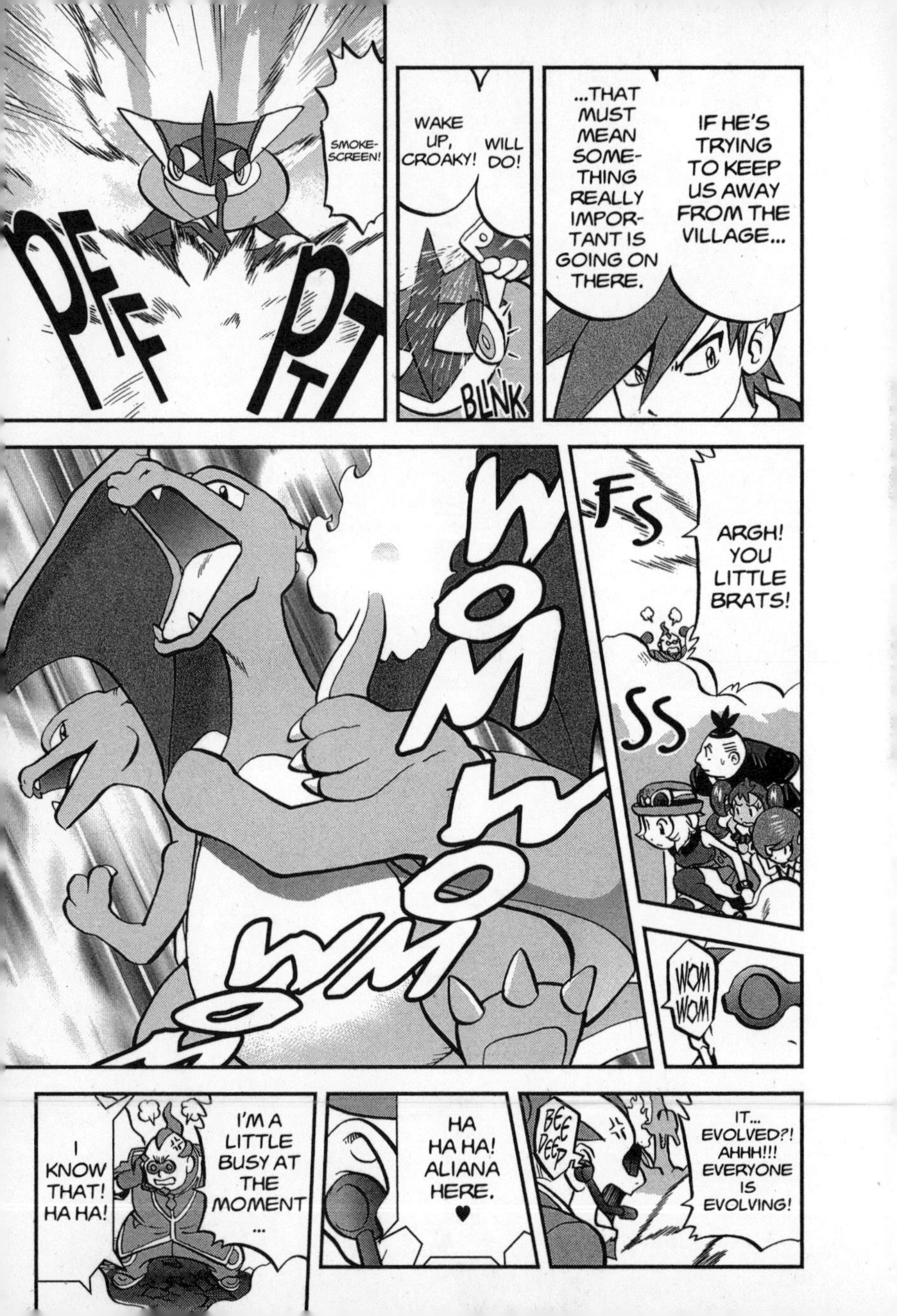
IF HE'S TRYING TO KEEP US AWAY FROM THE VILLAGE...
...THAT MUST MEAN SOMETHING REALLY IMPORTANT IS GOING ON THERE.
WILL DO!
WAKE UP, CROAKY!
BLINK
SMOKE-SCREEN!
PFFF
PTT
FS
ARGH! YOU LITTLE BRATS!
SS
WOM WOM
WOMWOMWOM
IT... EVOLVED?! AHHH!!! EVERYONE IS EVOLVING!
BEE DEEP
HA HA HA! ALIANA HERE. ♥
I'M A LITTLE BUSY AT THE MOMENT ...
I KNOW THAT! HA HA!

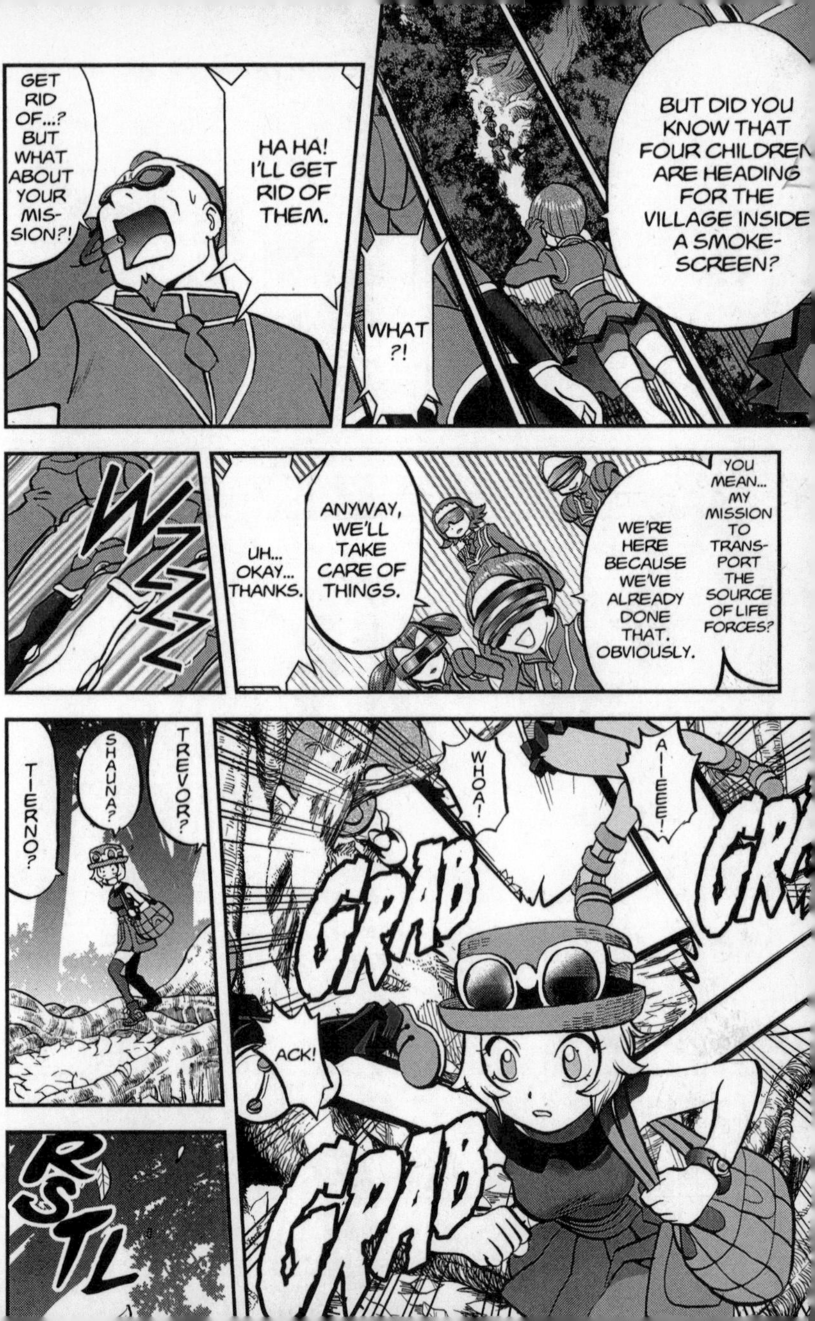
BUT DID YOU KNOW THAT FOUR CHILDREN ARE HEADING FOR THE VILLAGE INSIDE A SMOKE-SCREEN?
WHAT?!
HA HA! I'LL GET RID OF THEM.
GET RID OF...? BUT WHAT ABOUT YOUR MIS-SION?!
YOU MEAN... MY MISSION TO TRANS-PORT THE SOURCE OF LIFE FORCES?
WE'RE HERE BECAUSE WE'VE ALREADY DONE THAT. OBVIOUSLY.
ANYWAY, WE'LL TAKE CARE OF THINGS.
UH... OKAY... THANKS.
WZZZ
GRA
AIEEE!
WHOA!
GRAB
ACK!
GRAB
TREVOR?
SHAUNA?
TIERNO?
RSTL

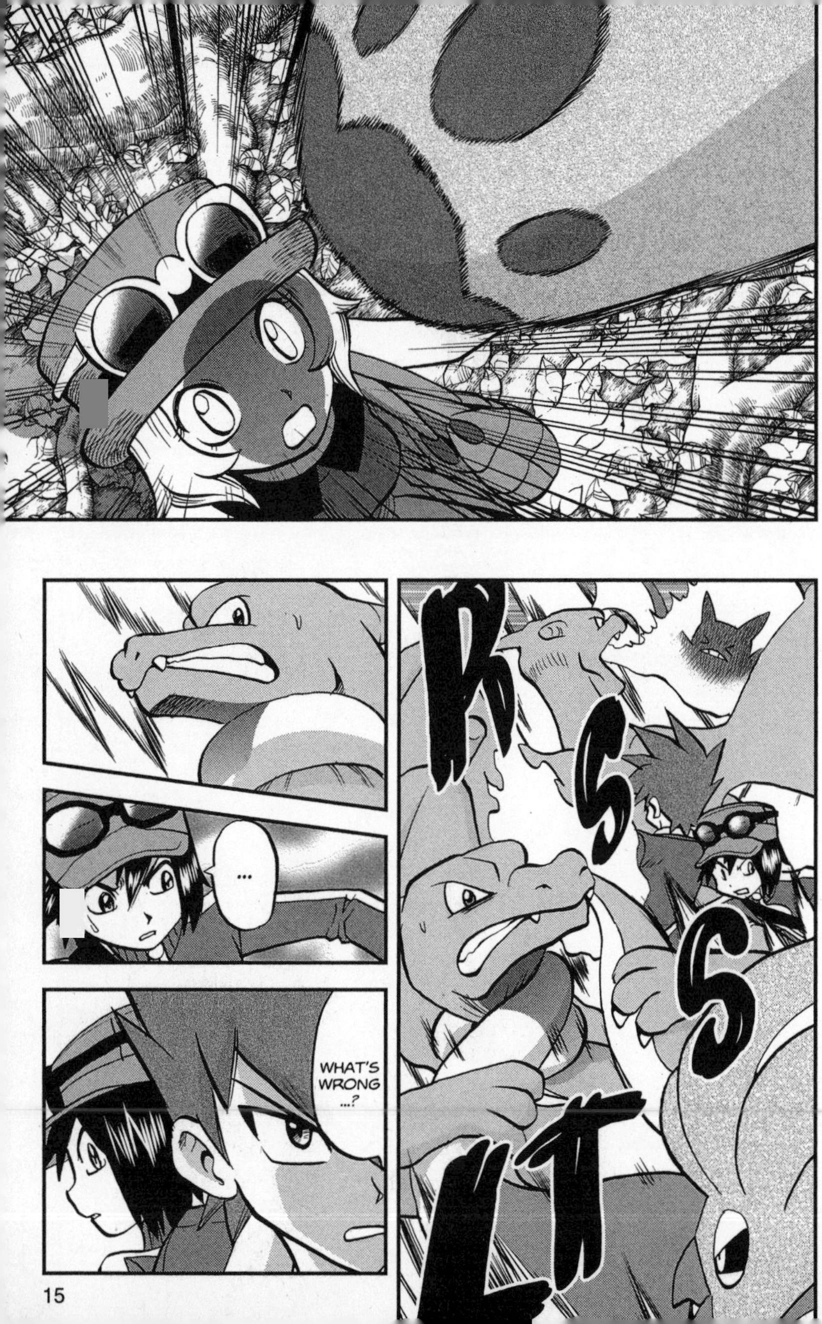
...
WHAT'S WRONG ...?

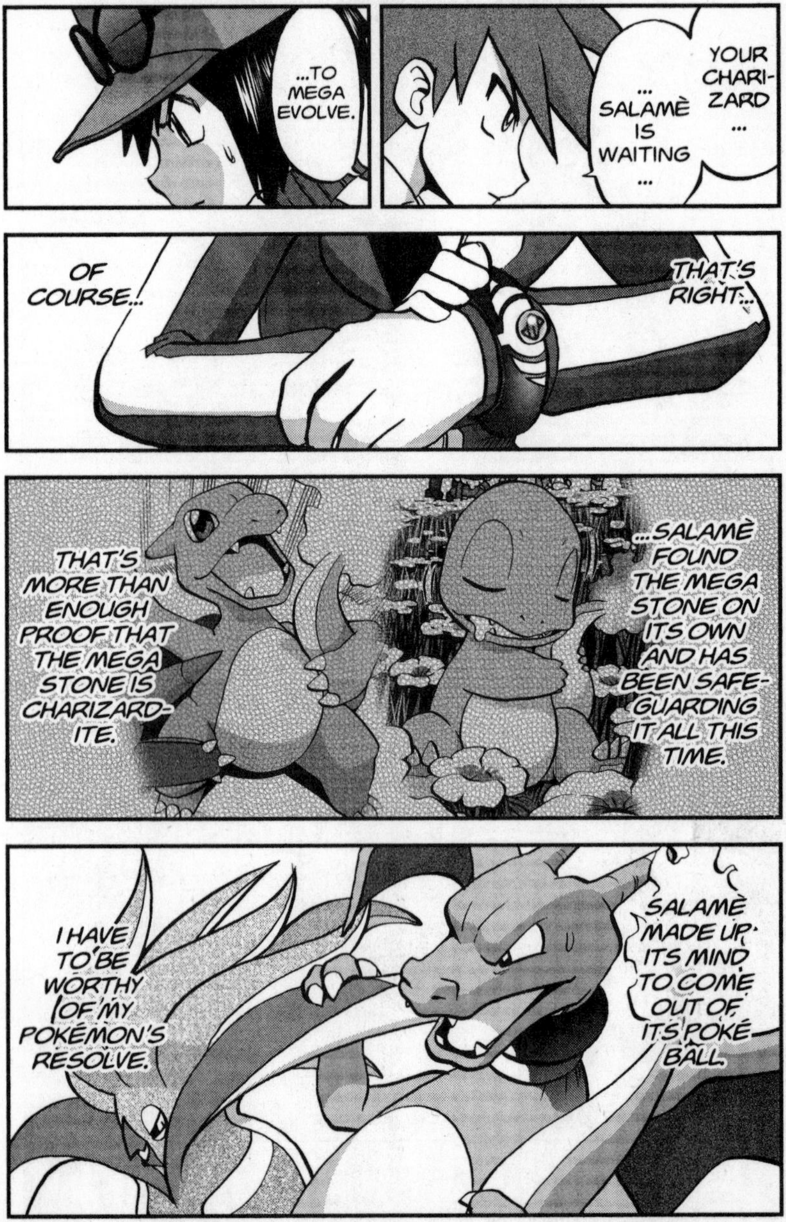
YOUR CHARI-ZARD ...
... SALAMÈ IS WAITING ...
...TO MEGA EVOLVE.
THAT'S RIGHT...
OF COURSE...
...SALAMÈ FOUND THE MEGA STONE ON ITS OWN AND HAS BEEN SAFE-GUARDING IT ALL THIS TIME.
THAT'S MORE THAN ENOUGH PROOF THAT THE MEGA STONE IS CHARIZARD-ITE.
SALAMÈ MADE UP ITS MIND TO COME OUT OF ITS POKÉ BALL.
I HAVE TO BE WORTHY OF MY POKÉMON'S RESOLVE.

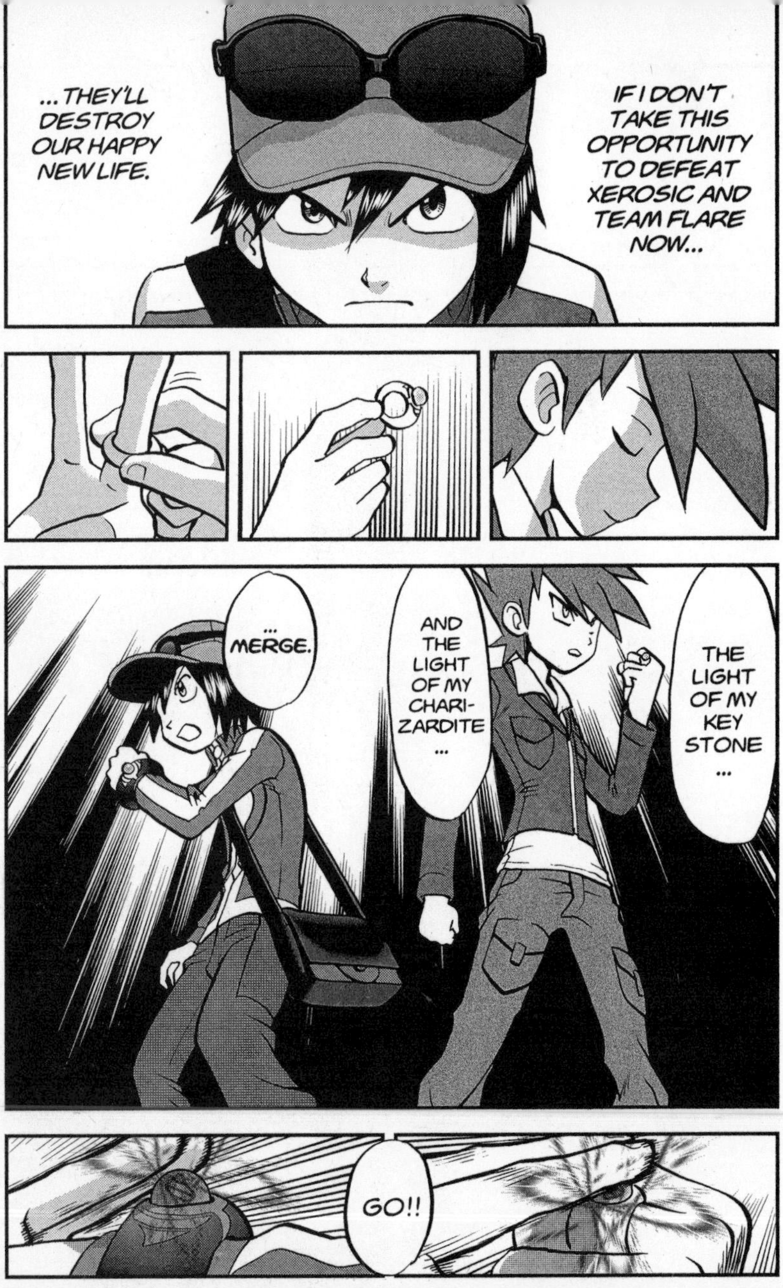
IF I DON'T TAKE THIS OPPORTUNITY TO DEFEAT XEROSIC AND TEAM FLARE NOW...
...THEY'LL DESTROY OUR HAPPY NEW LIFE.
THE LIGHT OF MY KEY STONE ...
AND THE LIGHT OF MY CHARI-ZARDITE ...
... MERGE.
GO!!

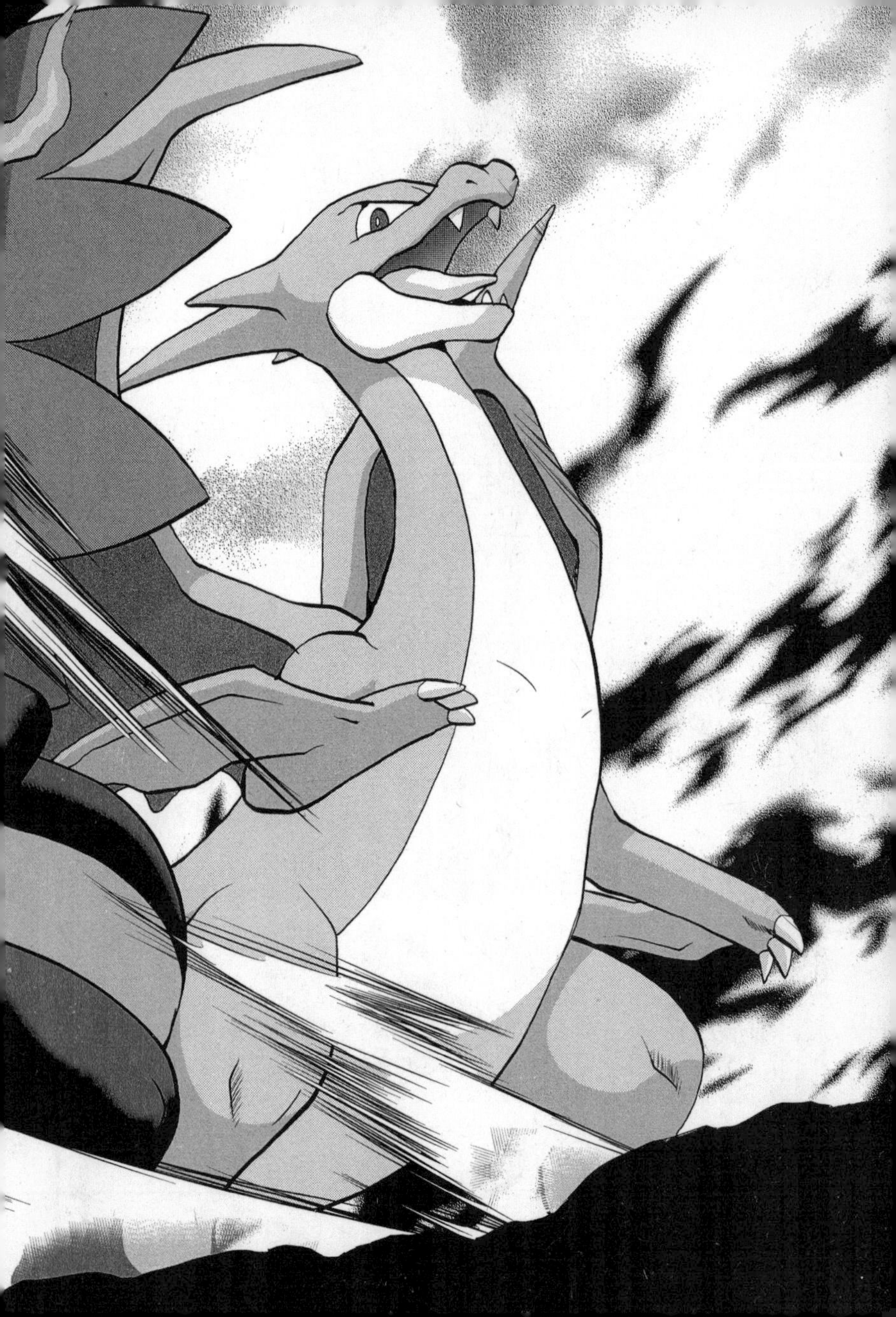

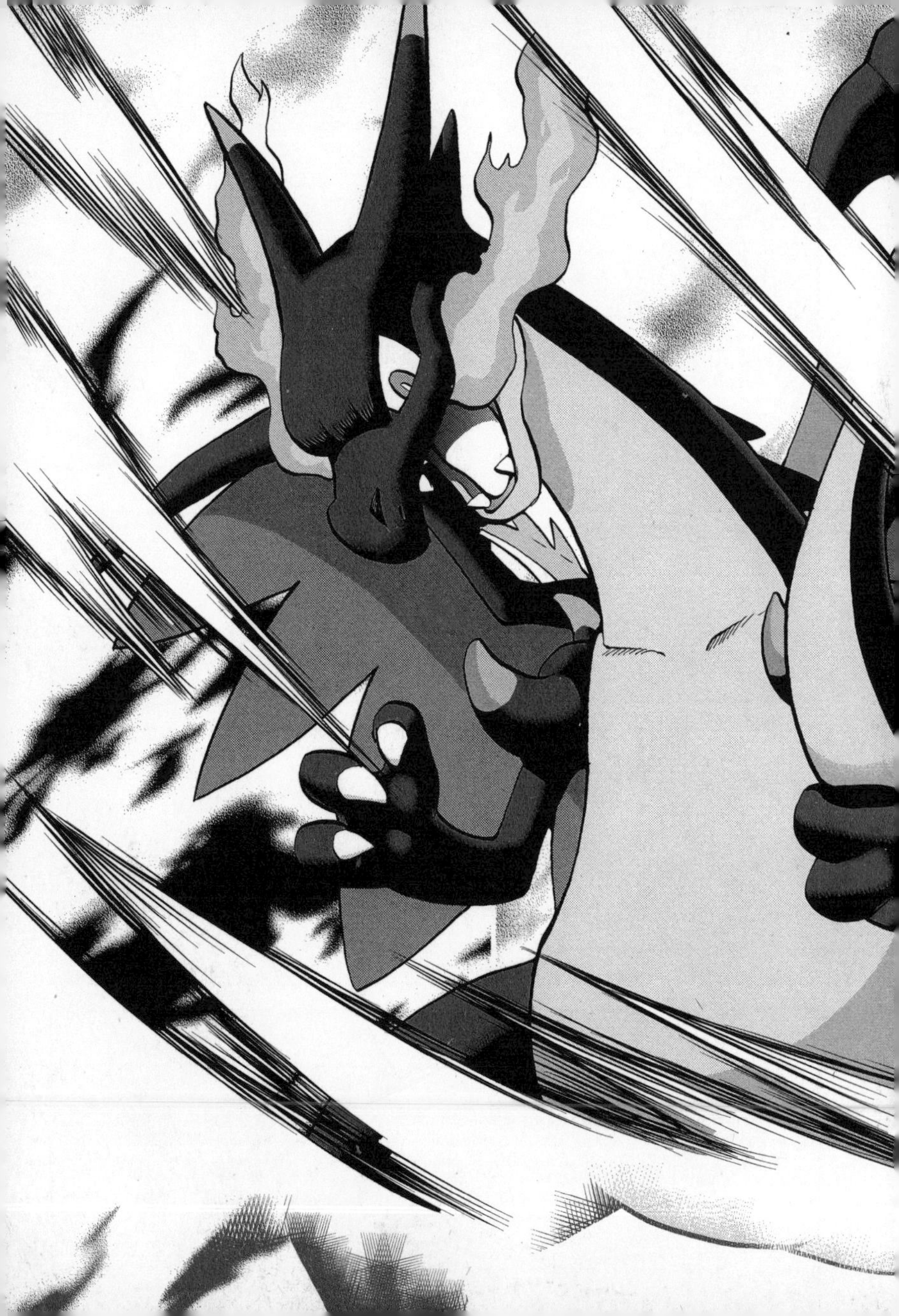

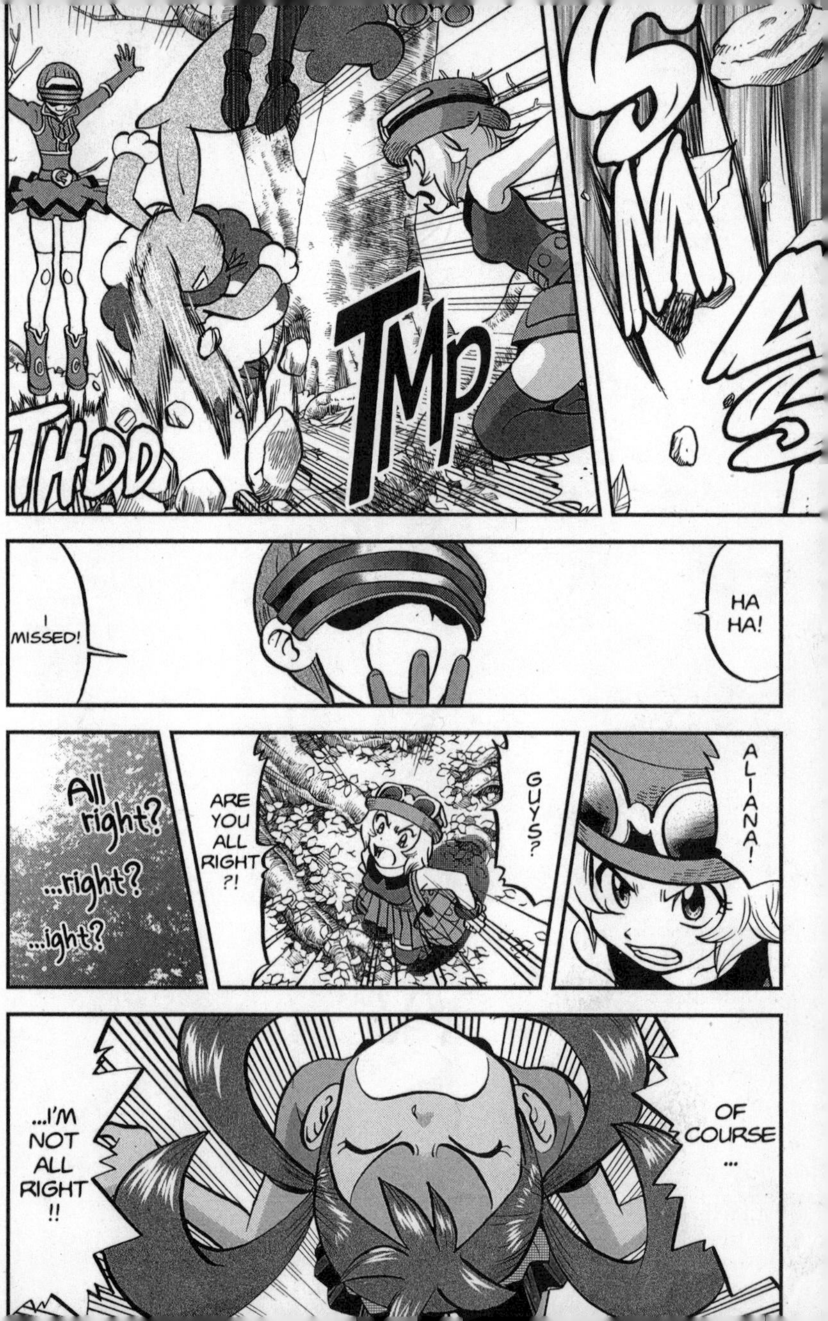
TMP
THDD
HA HA!
I MISSED!
ALIANA!
GUYS?
ARE YOU ALL RIGHT ?!
All right?
...right?
...ight?
OF COURSE ...
...I'M NOT ALL RIGHT !!

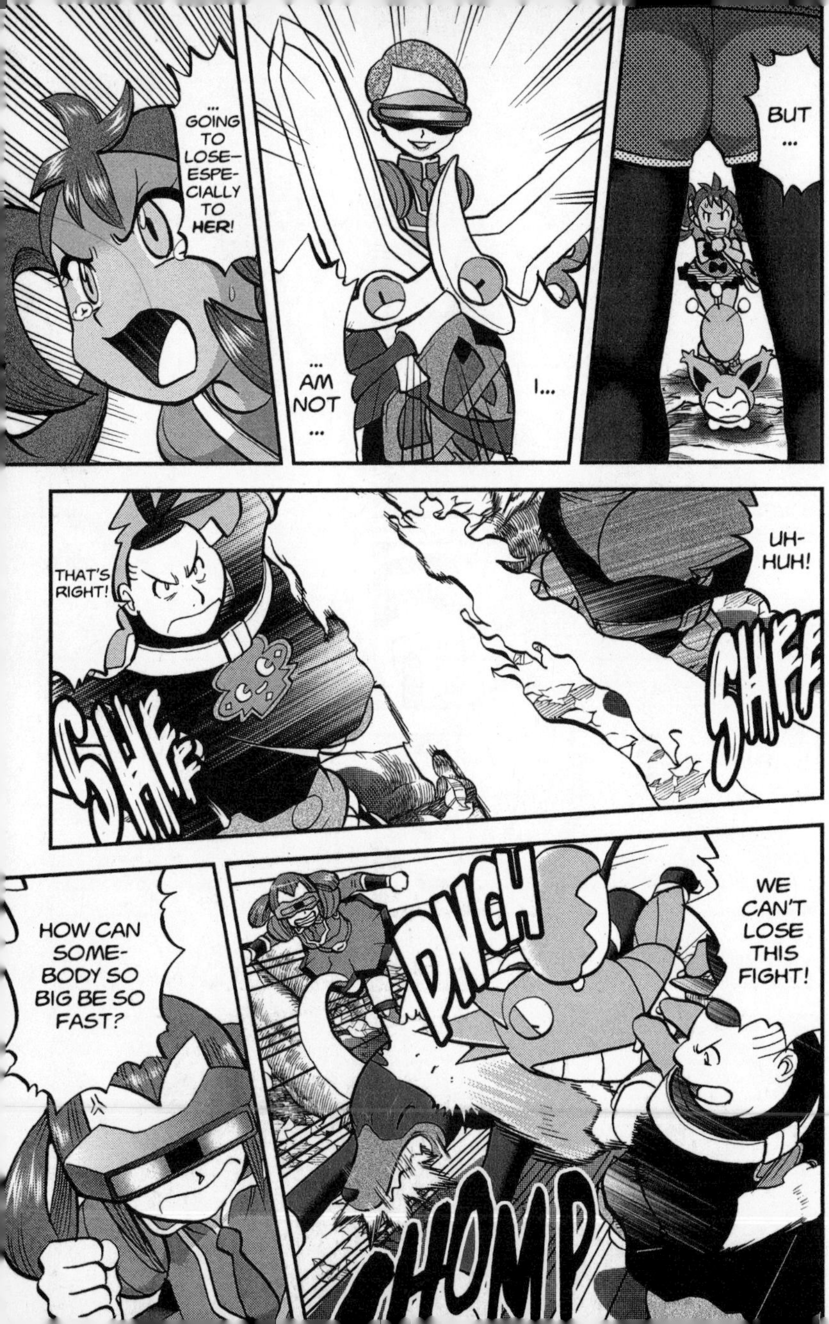
BUT ...
I...
... AM NOT ...
... GOING TO LOSE-ESPECIALLY TO HER!
UH-HUH!
SHFF
THAT'S RIGHT!
SHFF
WE CAN'T LOSE THIS FIGHT!
DNCH
HOMP
HOW CAN SOMEBODY SO BIG BE SO FAST?

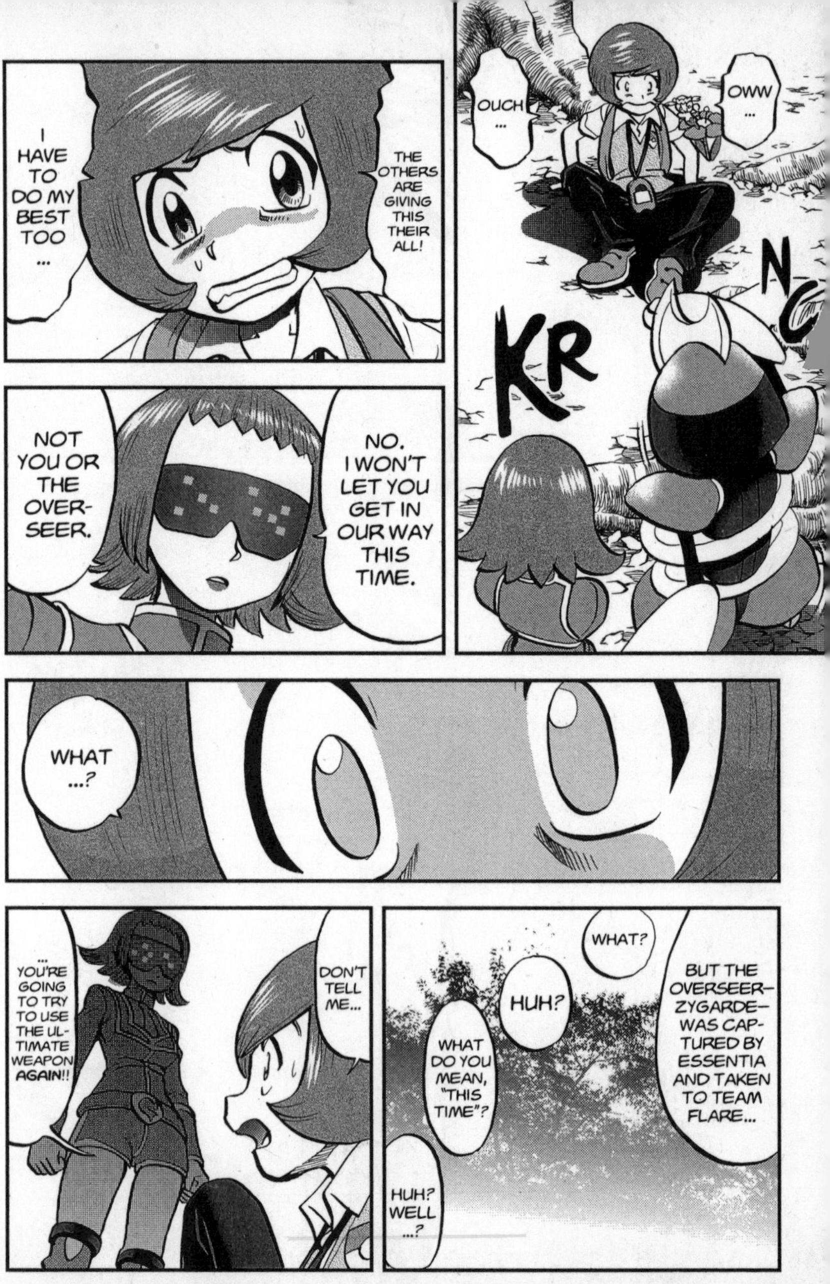
OWW...
OUCH...
KRNG
THE OTHERS ARE GIVING THIS THEIR ALL!
I HAVE TO DO MY BEST TOO...
NO. I WON'T LET YOU GET IN OUR WAY THIS TIME.
NOT YOU OR THE OVER-SEER.
WHAT...?
BUT THE OVERSEER—ZYGARDE—WAS CAPTURED BY ESSENTIA AND TAKEN TO TEAM FLARE...
WHAT?
HUH?
WHAT DO YOU MEAN, "THIS TIME"?
HUH? WELL...?
DON'T TELL ME...
...YOU'RE GOING TO TRY TO USE THE ULTIMATE WEAPON AGAIN!!

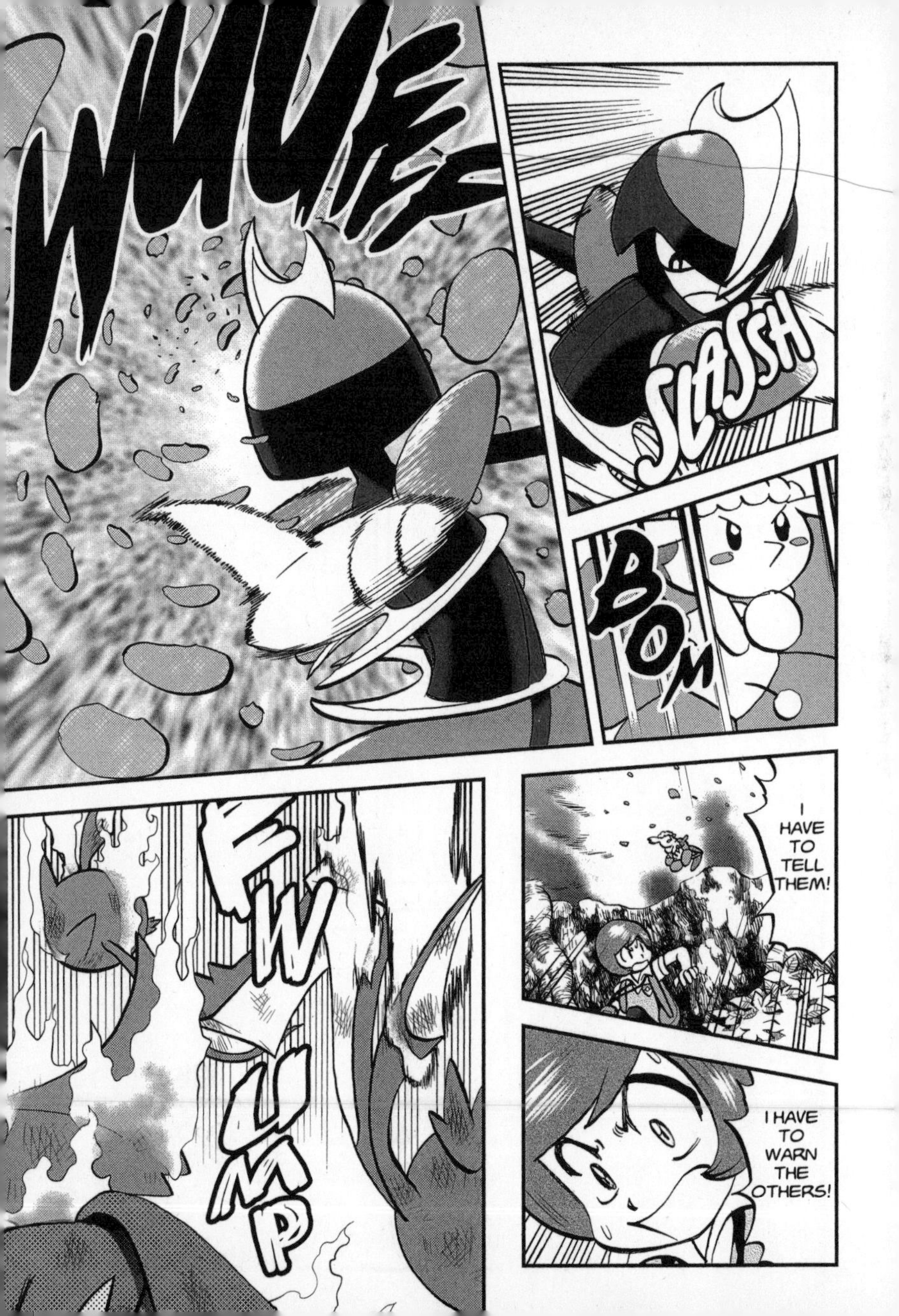
SLASSH
BOM
I HAVE TO TELL THEM!
I HAVE TO WARN THE OTHERS!
FWUMP

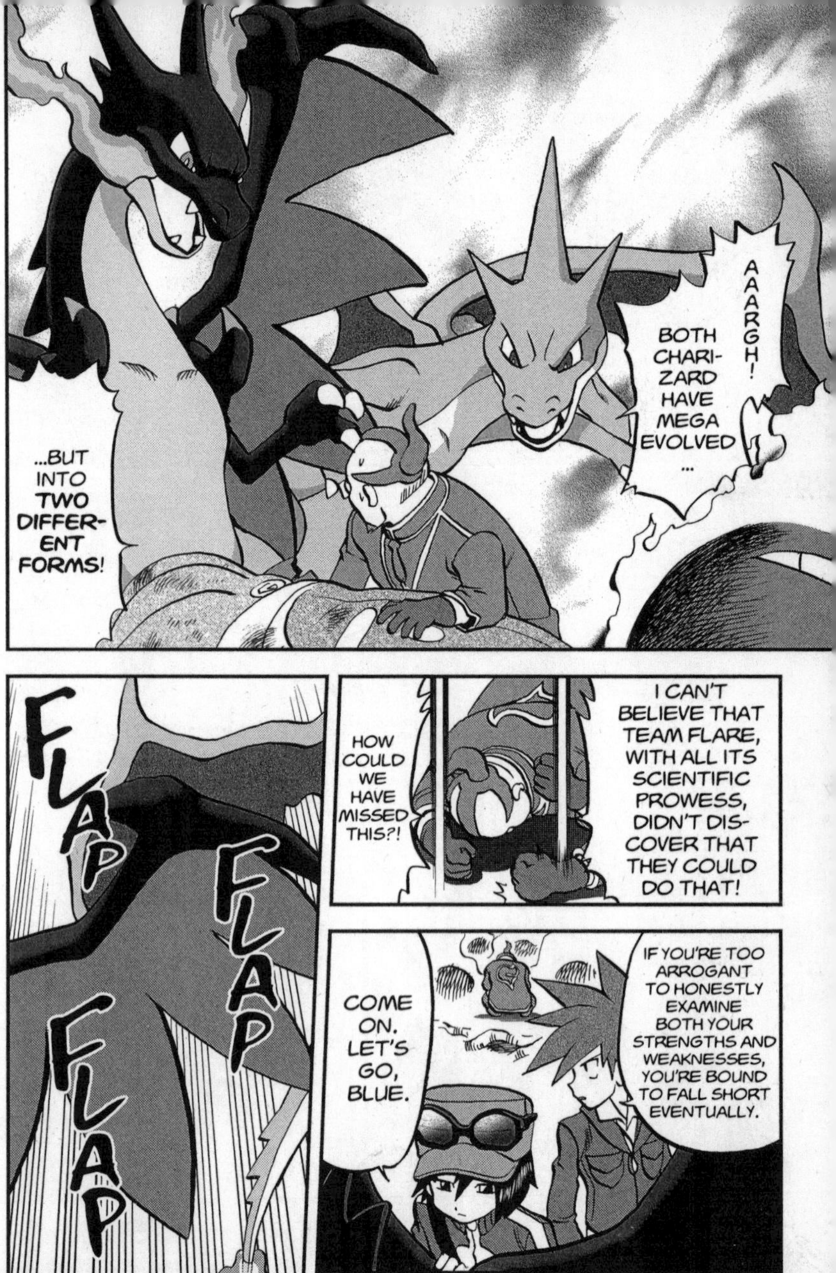
AAAARGH!
BOTH CHARIZARD HAVE MEGA EVOLVED...
...BUT INTO TWO DIFFERENT FORMS!
I CAN'T BELIEVE THAT TEAM FLARE, WITH ALL ITS SCIENTIFIC PROWESS, DIDN'T DISCOVER THAT THEY COULD DO THAT!
HOW COULD WE HAVE MISSED THIS?!
IF YOU'RE TOO ARROGANT TO HONESTLY EXAMINE BOTH YOUR STRENGTHS AND WEAKNESSES, YOU'RE BOUND TO FALL SHORT EVENTUALLY.
COME ON. LET'S GO, BLUE.
FLAP
FLAP
FLAP

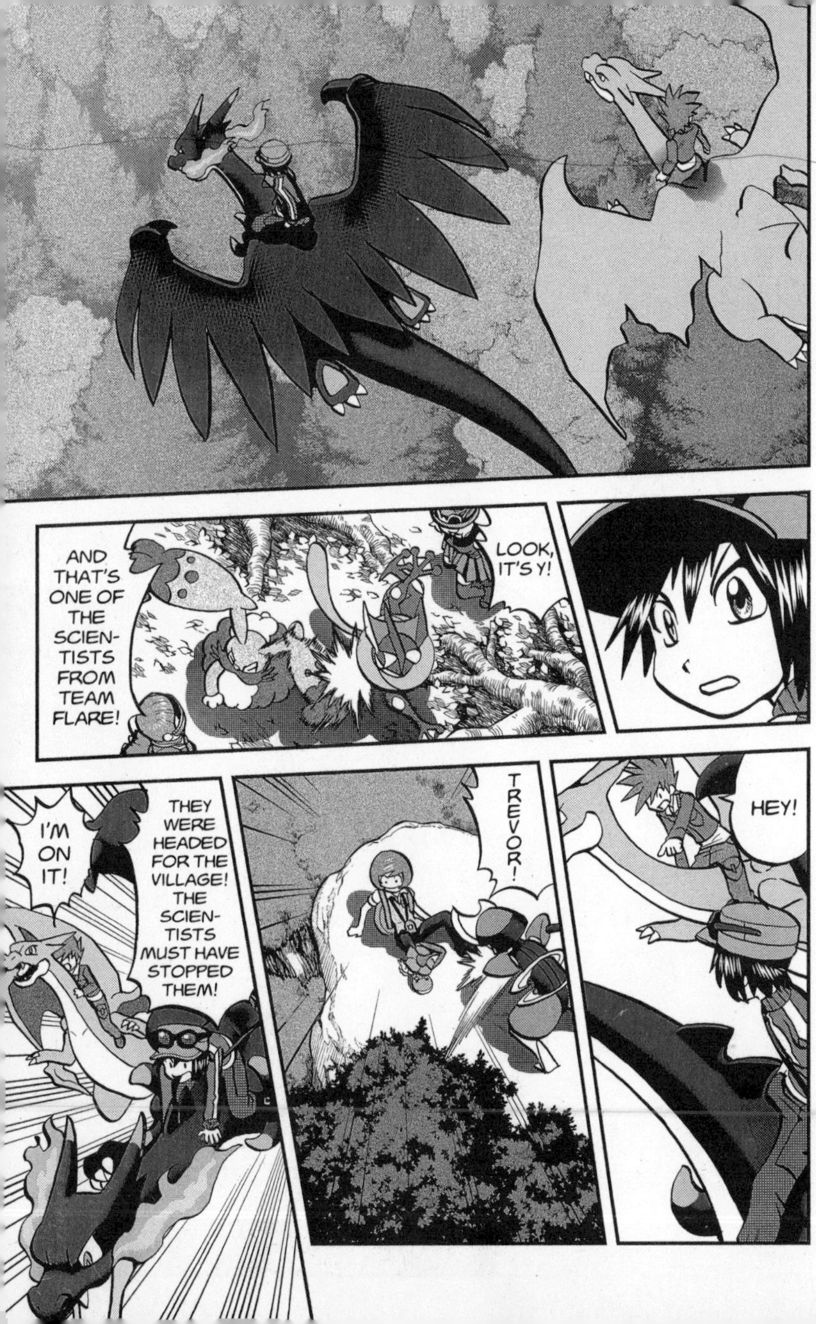
LOOK, IT'S Y!
AND THAT'S ONE OF THE SCIENTISTS FROM TEAM FLARE!
HEY!
TREVOR!
THEY WERE HEADED FOR THE VILLAGE! THE SCIENTISTS MUST HAVE STOPPED THEM!
I'M ON IT!

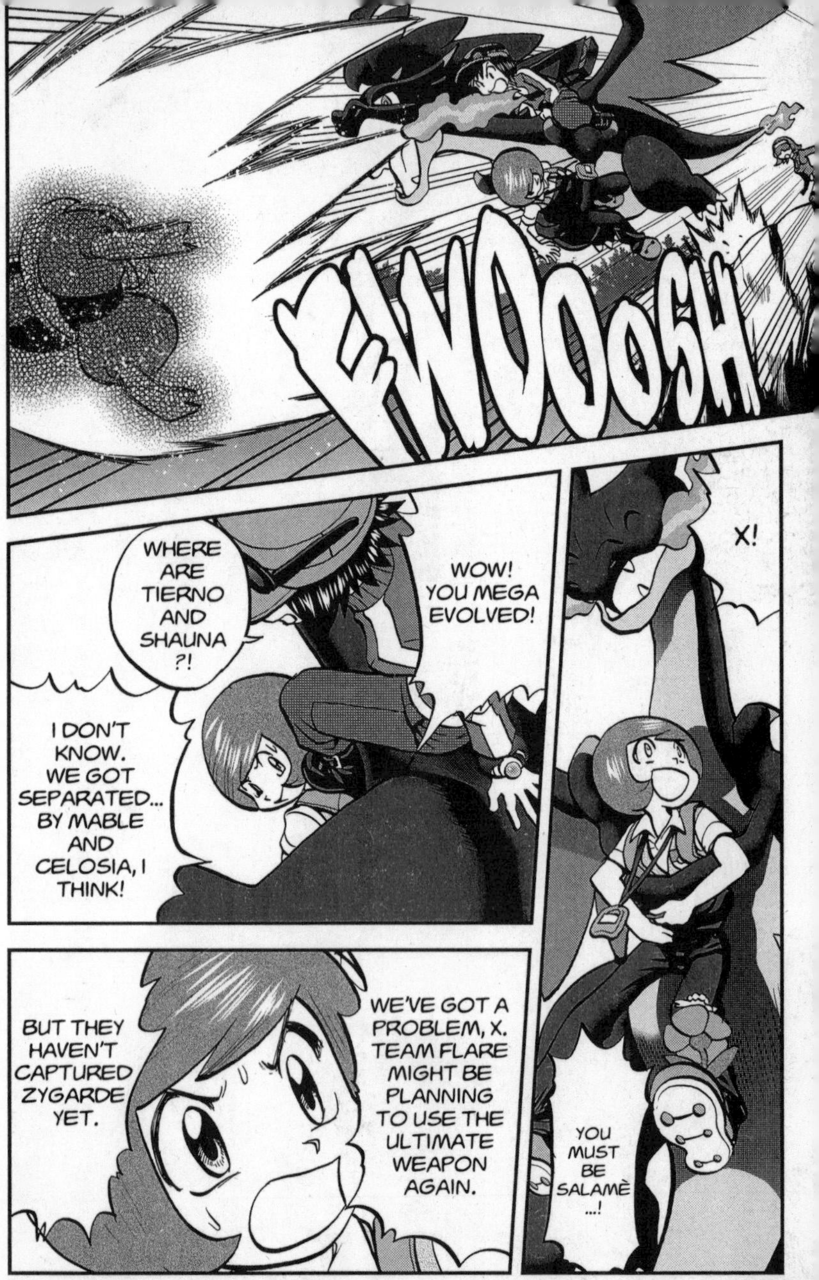
WHOOOSH
X!
YOU MUST BE SALAMÈ ...!
WOW! YOU MEGA EVOLVED!
WHERE ARE TIERNO AND SHAUNA ?!
I DON'T KNOW. WE GOT SEPARATED... BY MABLE AND CELOSIA, I THINK!
WE'VE GOT A PROBLEM, X. TEAM FLARE MIGHT BE PLANNING TO USE THE ULTIMATE WEAPON AGAIN.
BUT THEY HAVEN'T CAPTURED ZYGARDE YET.

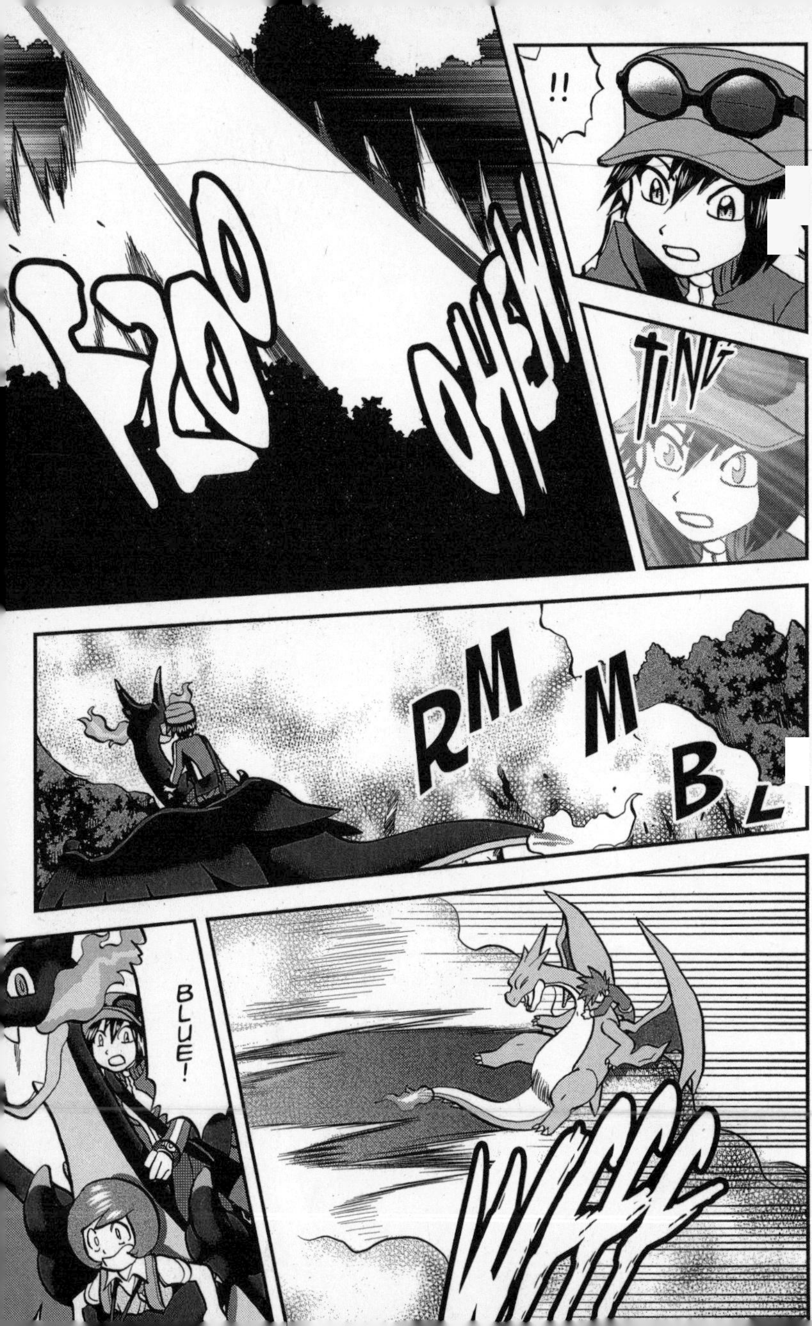
!!
TINT
RM M BL
BLUE!

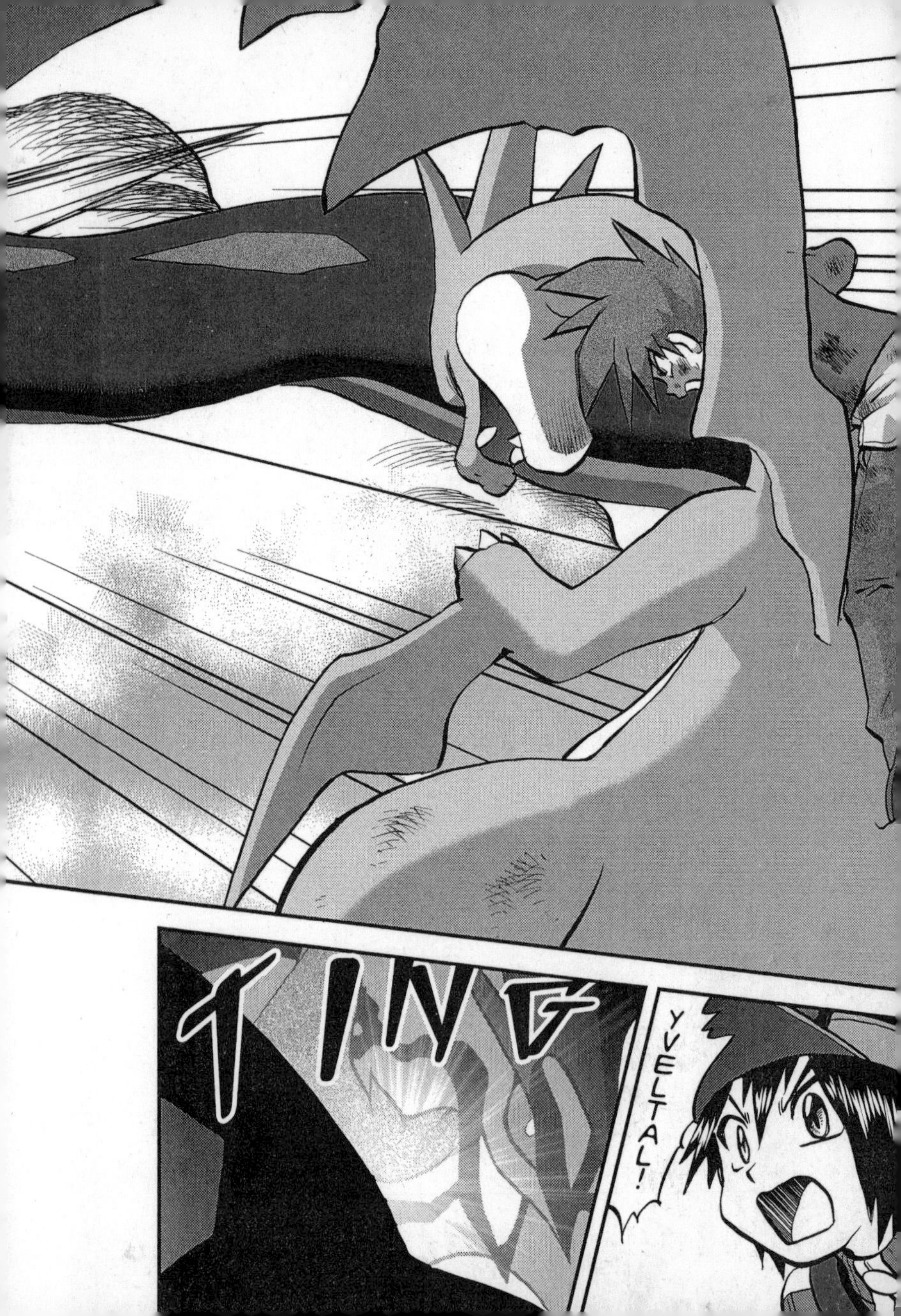
TING
YVELTAL!

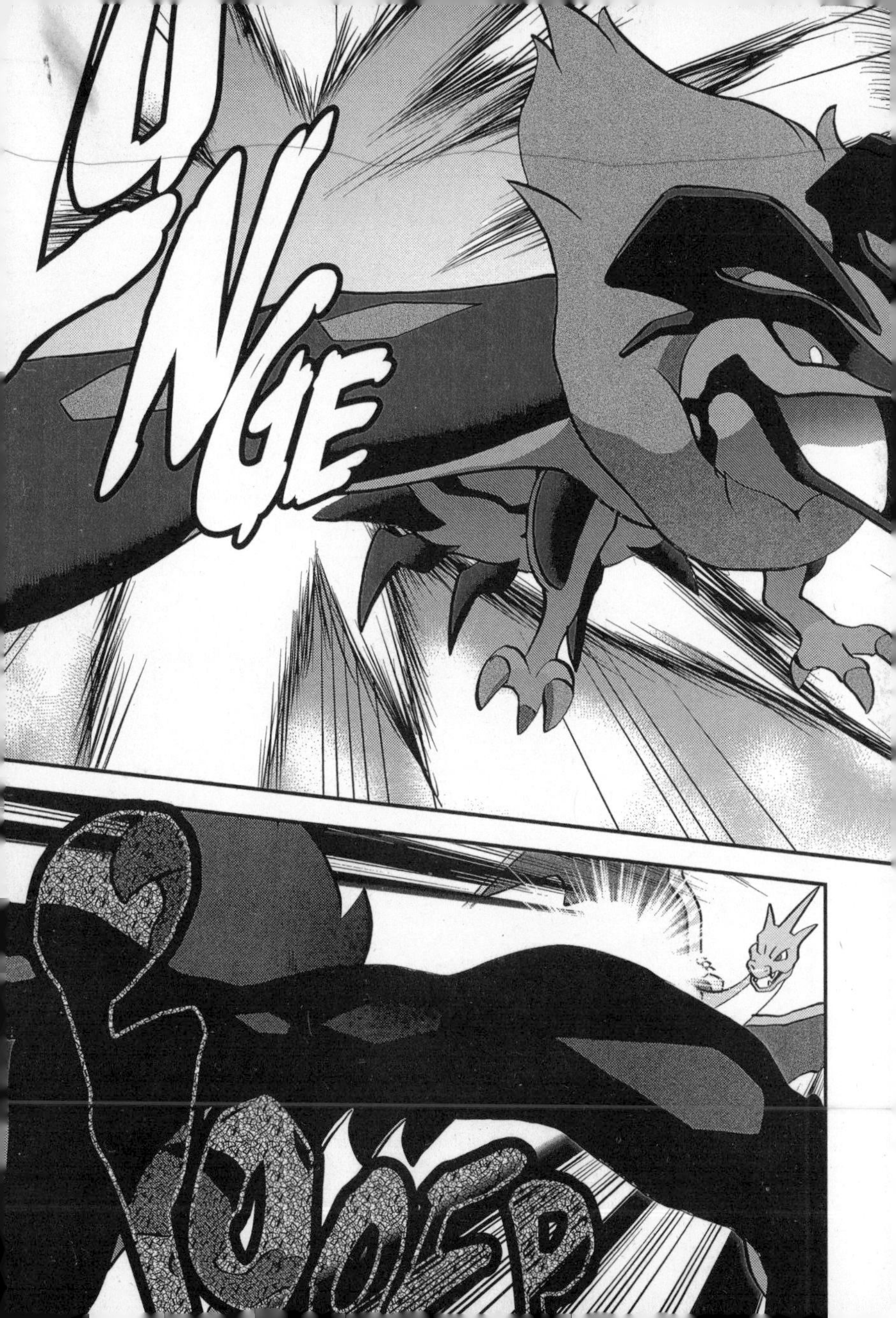
NGE

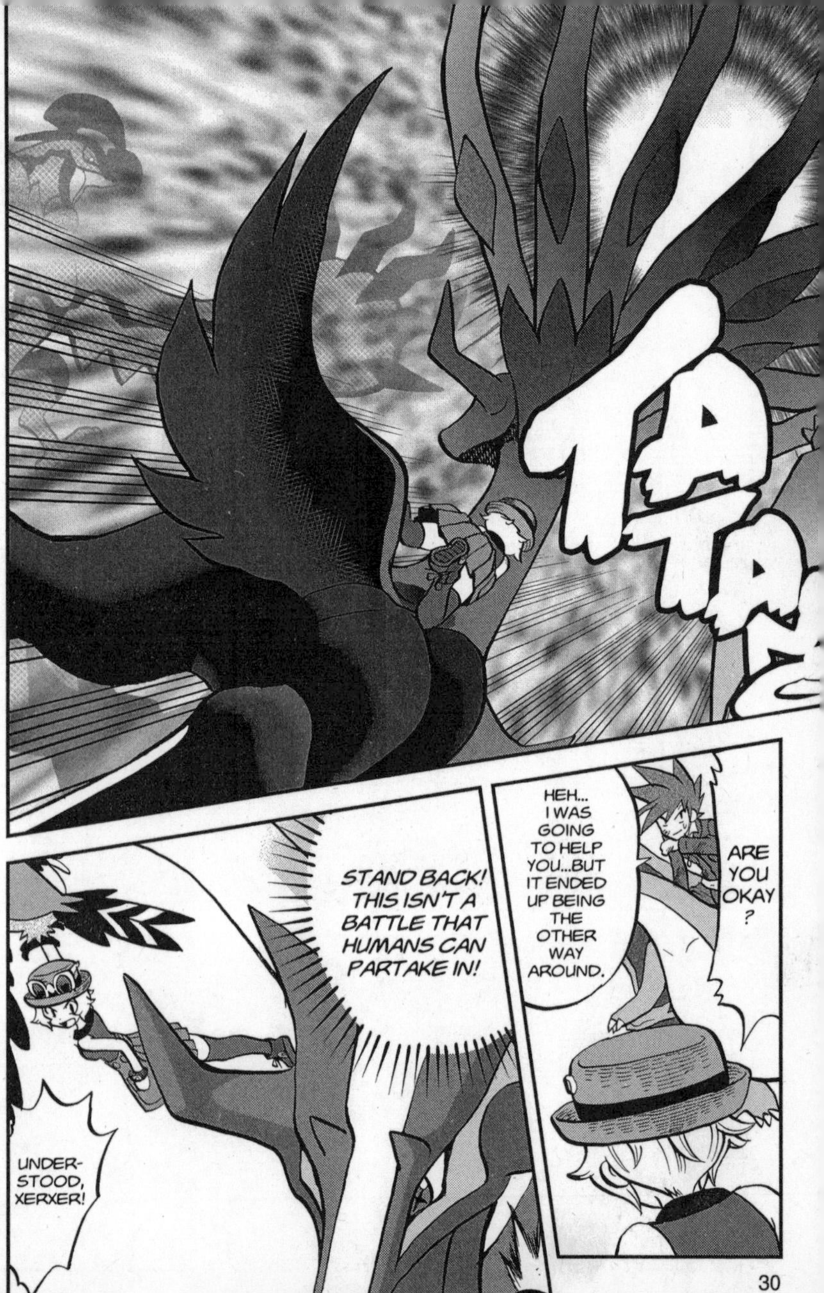
TA
TA
ARE YOU OKAY?
HEH... I WAS GOING TO HELP YOU...BUT IT ENDED UP BEING THE OTHER WAY AROUND.
STAND BACK! THIS ISN'T A BATTLE THAT HUMANS CAN PARTAKE IN!
UNDER-STOOD, XERXER!

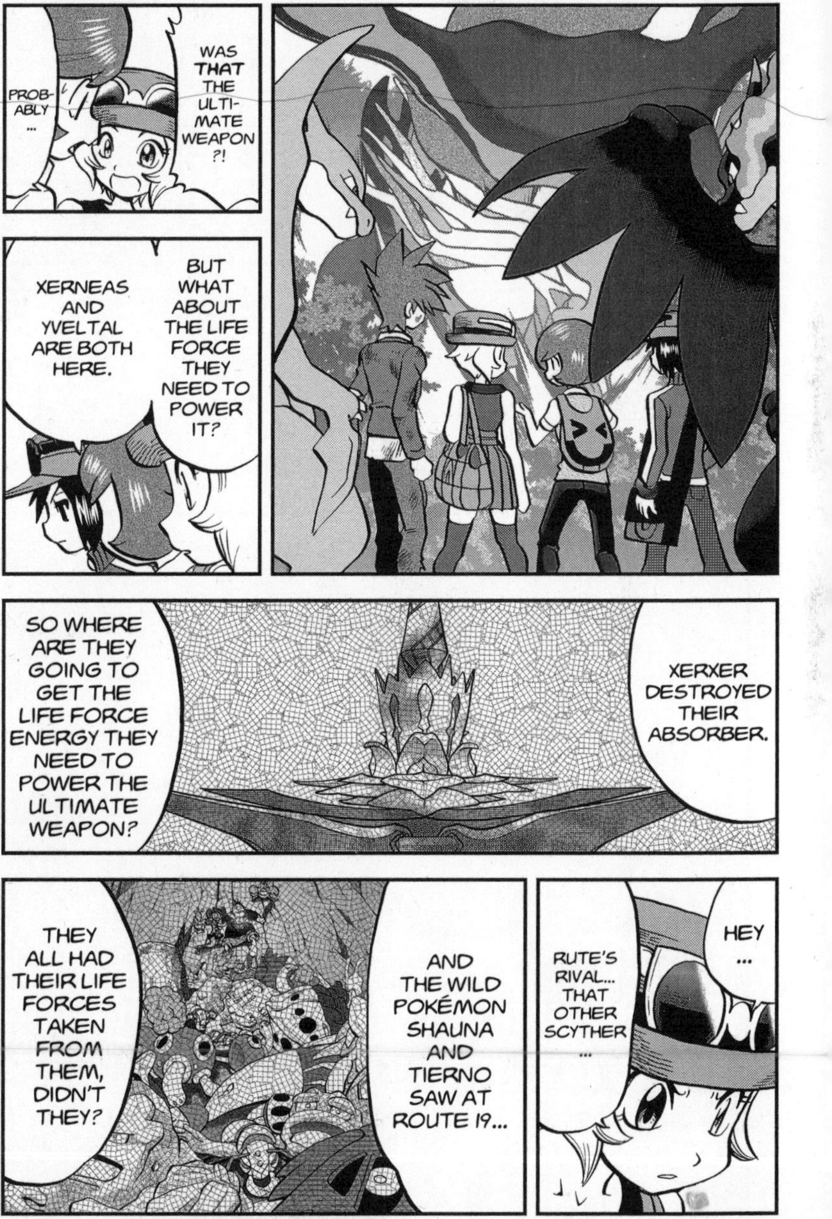
WAS THAT THE ULTIMATE WEAPON ?!
PROBABLY ...
BUT WHAT ABOUT THE LIFE FORCE THEY NEED TO POWER IT?
XERNEAS AND YVELTAL ARE BOTH HERE.
XERXER DESTROYED THEIR ABSORBER.
SO WHERE ARE THEY GOING TO GET THE LIFE FORCE ENERGY THEY NEED TO POWER THE ULTIMATE WEAPON?
HEY ...
RUTE'S RIVAL... THAT OTHER SCYTHER ...
AND THE WILD POKÉMON SHAUNA AND TIERNO SAW AT ROUTE 19...
THEY ALL HAD THEIR LIFE FORCES TAKEN FROM THEM, DIDN'T THEY?

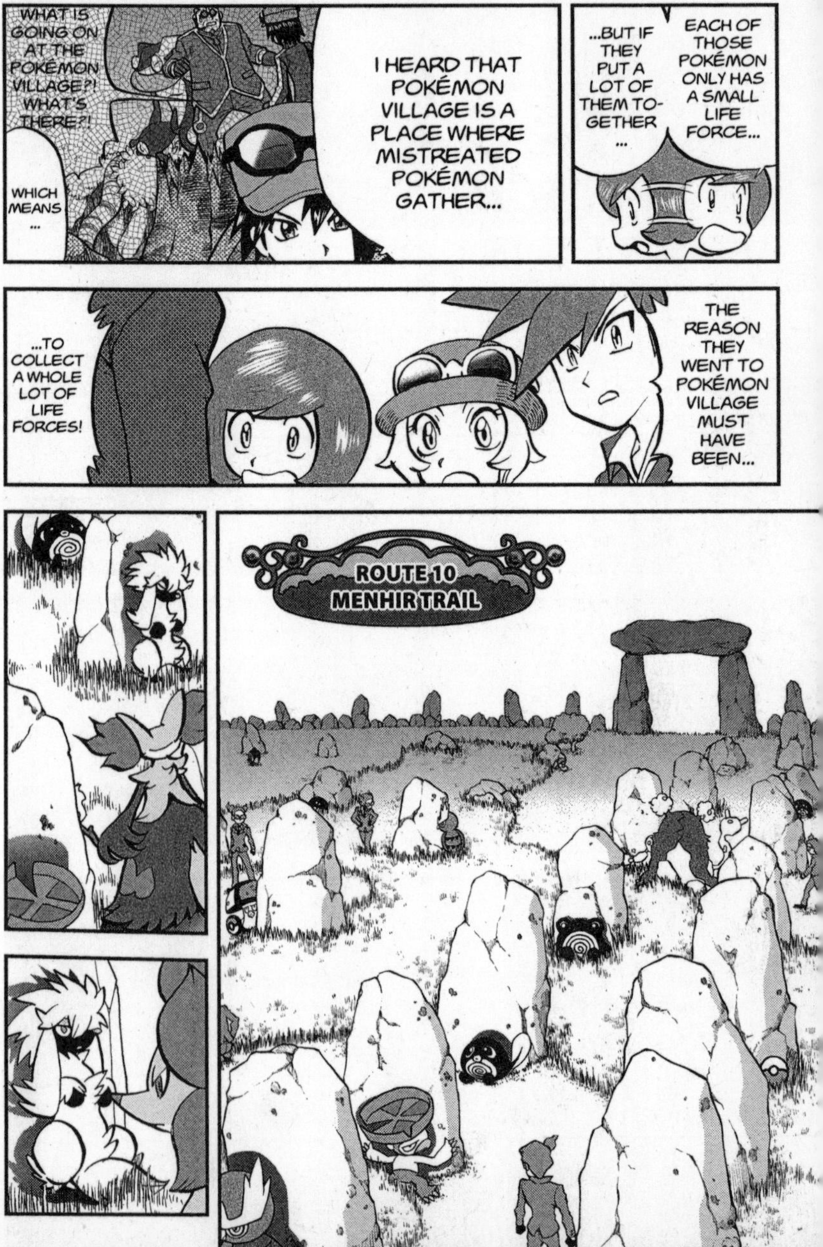
EACH OF THOSE POKÉMON ONLY HAS A SMALL LIFE FORCE...
...BUT IF THEY PUT A LOT OF THEM TO-GETHER ...
I HEARD THAT POKÉMON VILLAGE IS A PLACE WHERE MISTREATED POKÉMON GATHER...
WHAT IS GOING ON AT THE POKÉMON VILLAGE?! WHAT'S THERE?!
WHICH MEANS ...
THE REASON THEY WENT TO POKÉMON VILLAGE MUST HAVE BEEN...
...TO COLLECT A WHOLE LOT OF LIFE FORCES!
ROUTE 10
MENHIR TRAIL

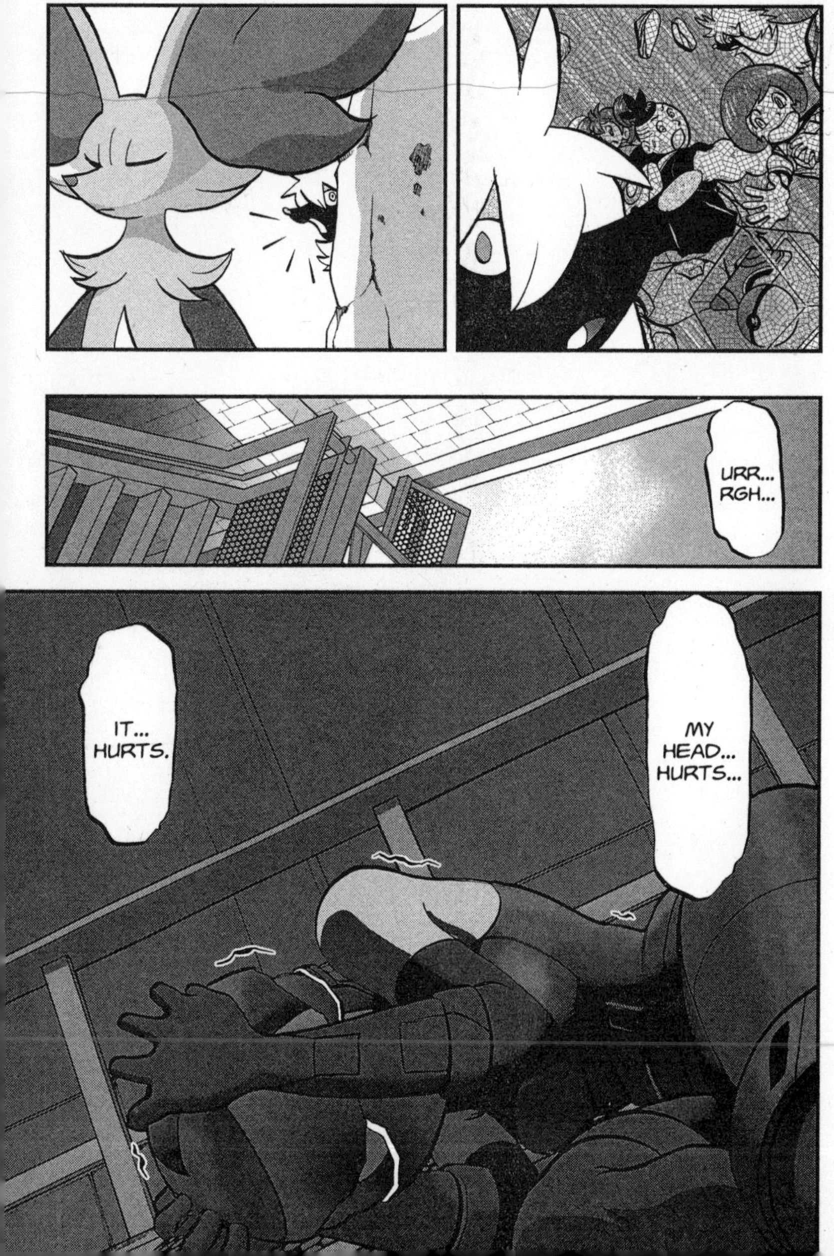
URR... RGH...
MY HEAD... HURTS...
IT... HURTS.

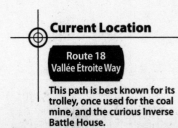

Current Location

Route 18
Vallée Étroite Way

This path is best known for its trolley, once used for the coal mine, and the curious Inverse Battle House.

Adventure 35 Yveltal Steals

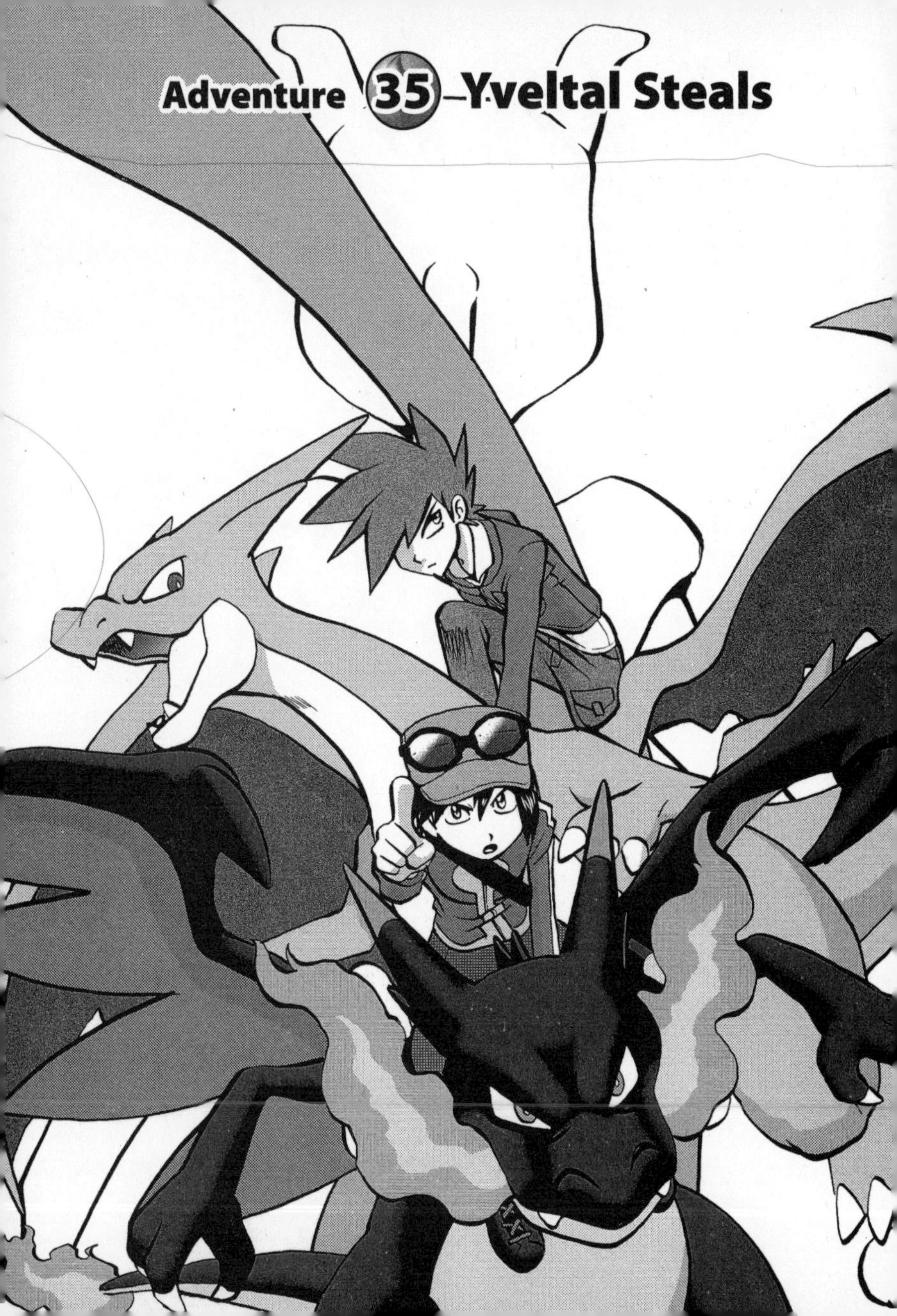

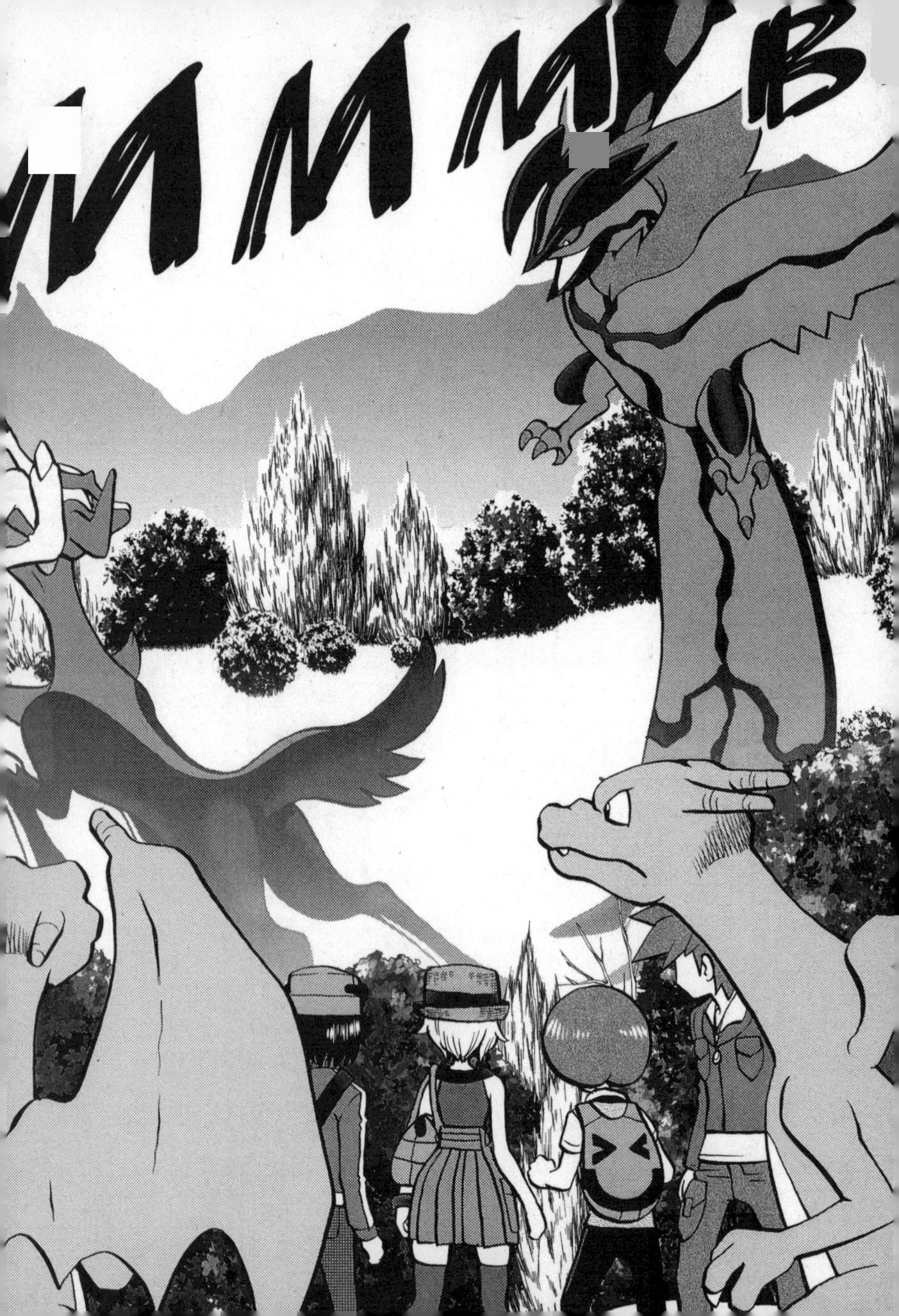

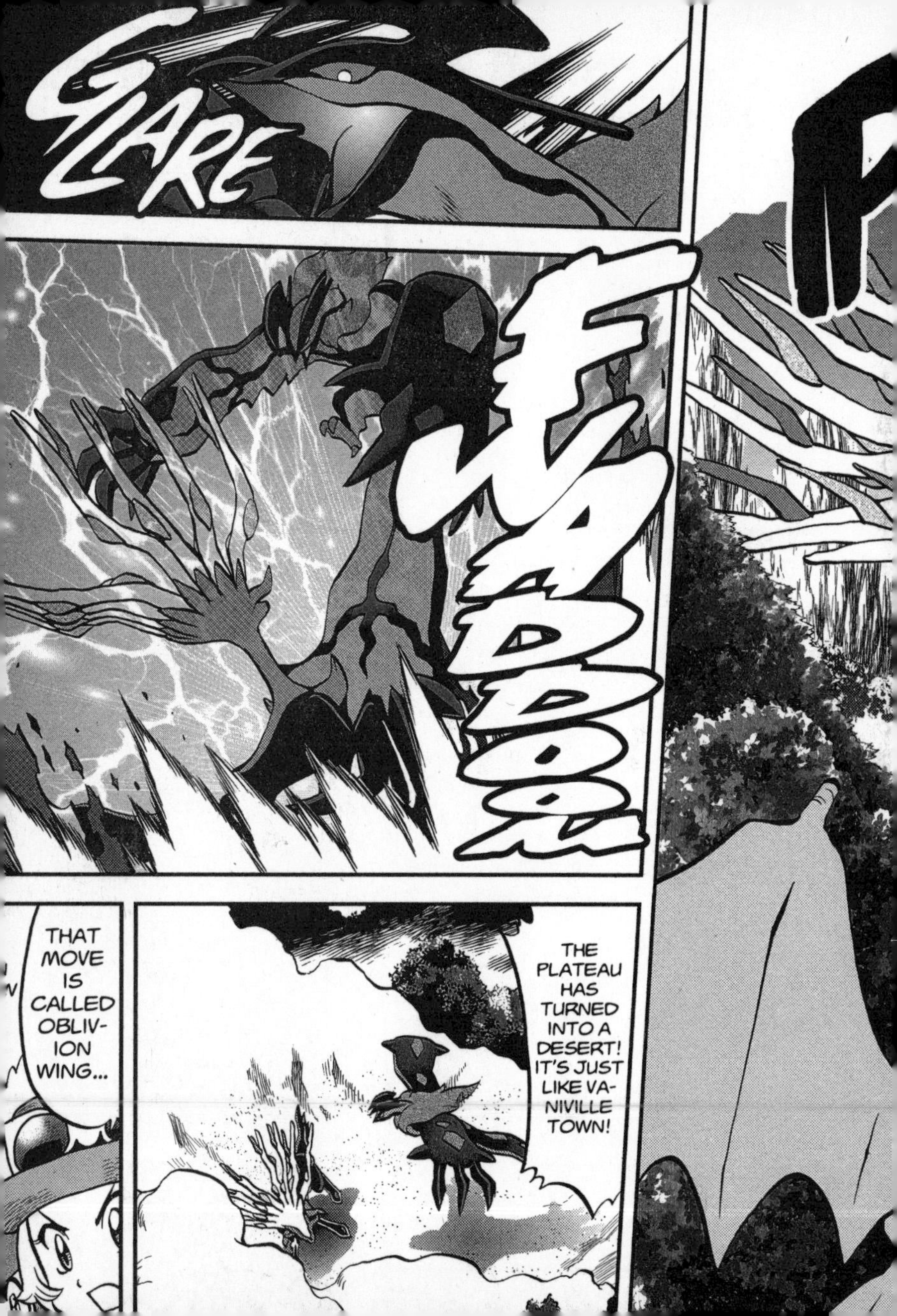
GLARE
THE PLATEAU HAS TURNED INTO A DESERT! IT'S JUST LIKE VA-NIVILLE TOWN!
THAT MOVE IS CALLED OBLIV-ION WING...

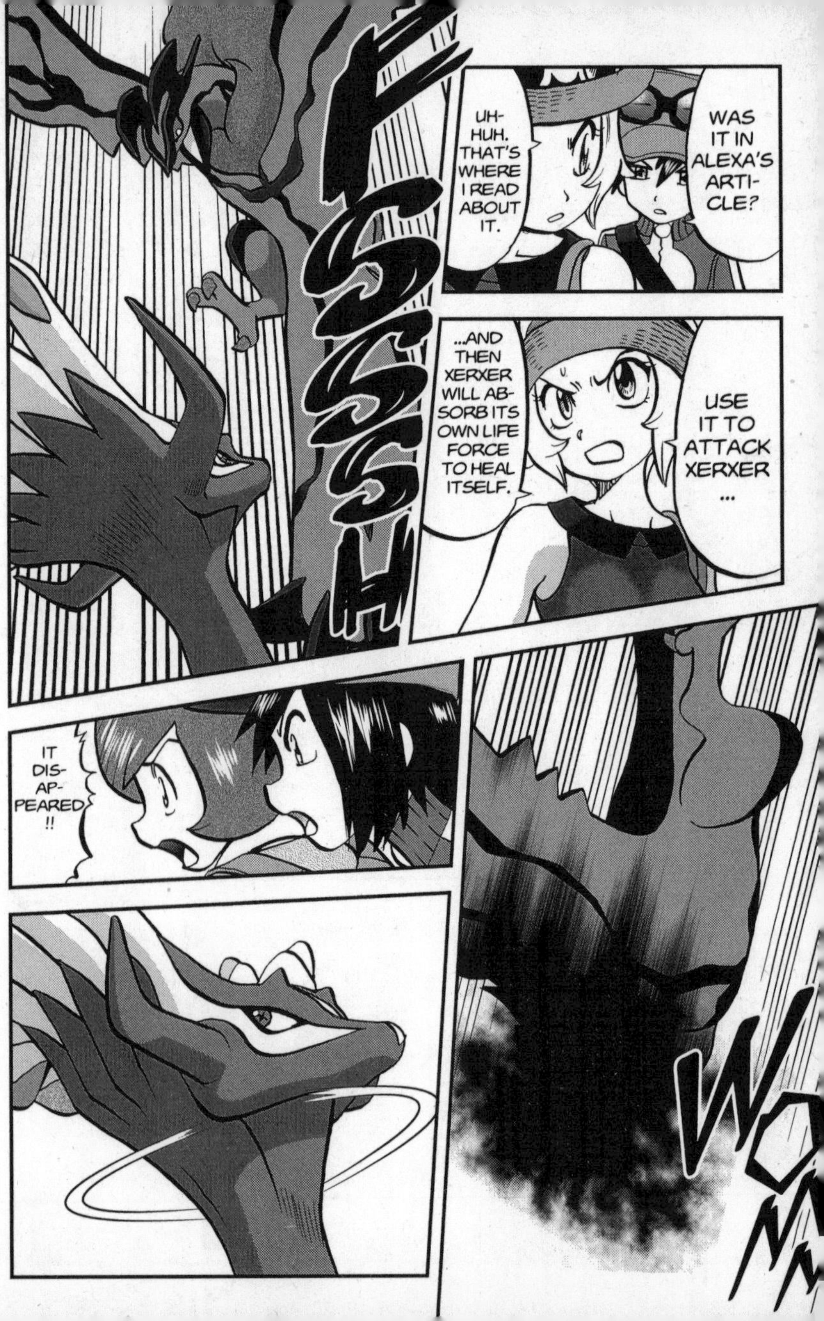
WAS IT IN ALEXA'S ARTI-CLE?
UH-HUH. THAT'S WHERE I READ ABOUT IT.
USE IT TO ATTACK XERXER ...
...AND THEN XERXER WILL AB-SORB ITS OWN LIFE FORCE TO HEAL ITSELF.
FSSSSH
WOMM
IT DIS-AP-PEARED!!

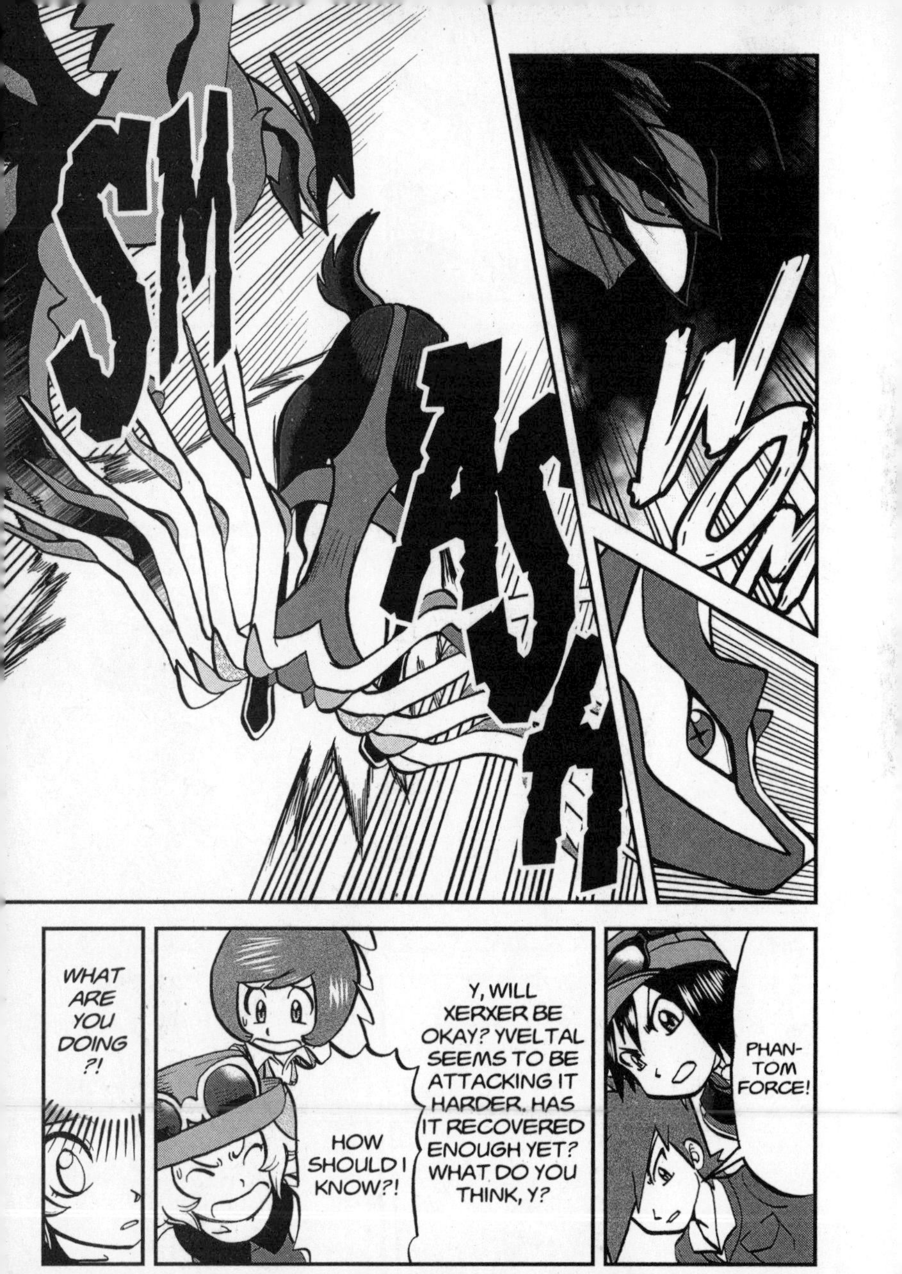
WOM
SMASH
PHAN-TOM FORCE!
Y, WILL XERXER BE OKAY? YVELTAL SEEMS TO BE ATTACKING IT HARDER. HAS IT RECOVERED ENOUGH YET? WHAT DO YOU THINK, Y?
HOW SHOULD I KNOW?!
WHAT ARE YOU DOING?!

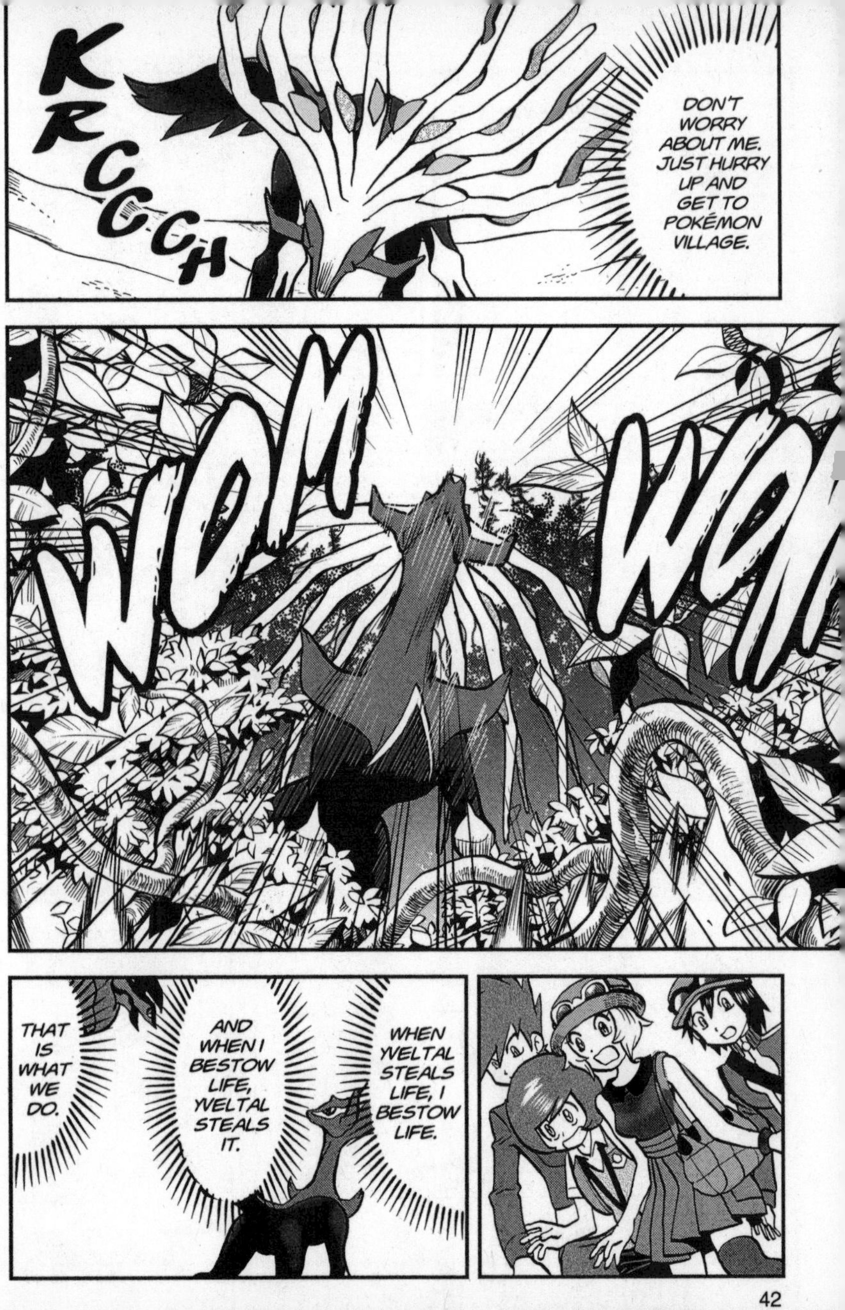
DON'T WORRY ABOUT ME. JUST HURRY UP AND GET TO POKÉMON VILLAGE.
KRCCCH
WOM
WHEN YVELTAL STEALS LIFE, I BESTOW LIFE.
AND WHEN I BESTOW LIFE, YVELTAL STEALS IT.
THAT IS WHAT WE DO.

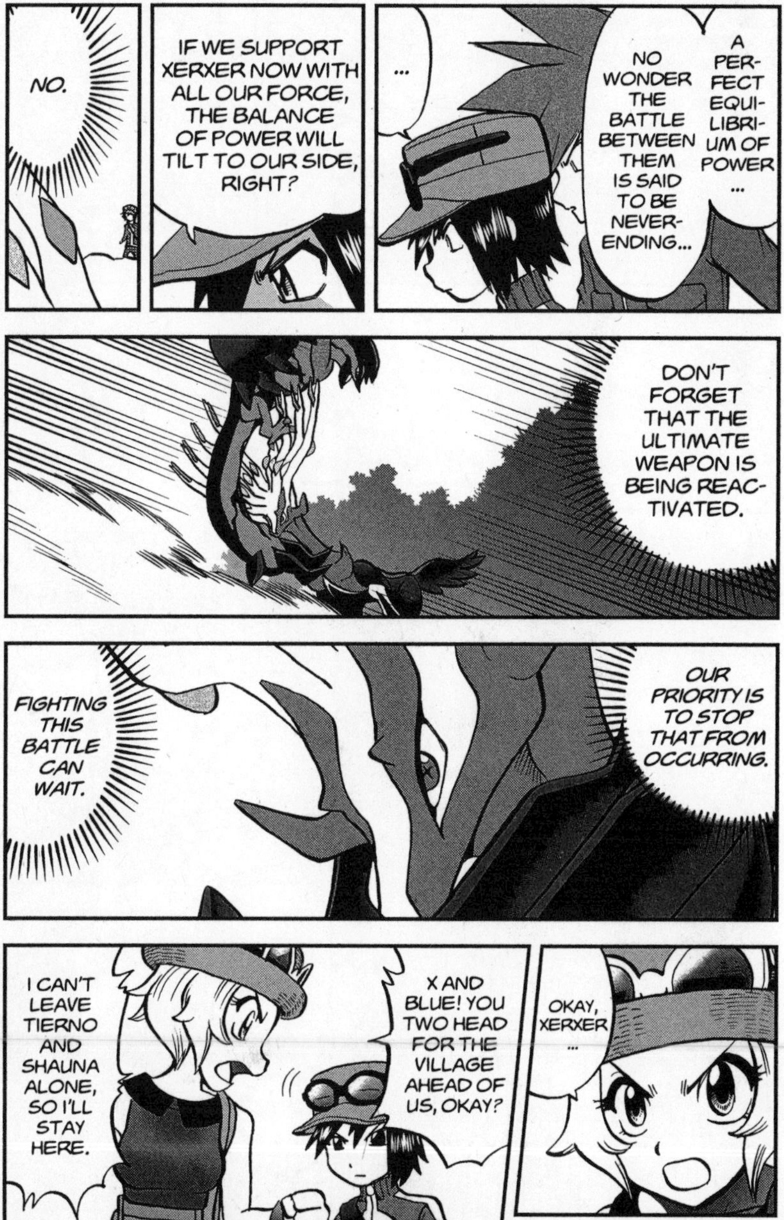
A PERFECT EQUILIBRIUM OF POWER...
NO WONDER THE BATTLE BETWEEN THEM IS SAID TO BE NEVER-ENDING...
...
IF WE SUPPORT XERXER NOW WITH ALL OUR FORCE, THE BALANCE OF POWER WILL TILT TO OUR SIDE, RIGHT?
NO.
DON'T FORGET THAT THE ULTIMATE WEAPON IS BEING REACTIVATED.
OUR PRIORITY IS TO STOP THAT FROM OCCURRING.
FIGHTING THIS BATTLE CAN WAIT.
OKAY, XERXER...
X AND BLUE! YOU TWO HEAD FOR THE VILLAGE AHEAD OF US, OKAY?
I CAN'T LEAVE TIERNO AND SHAUNA ALONE, SO I'LL STAY HERE.

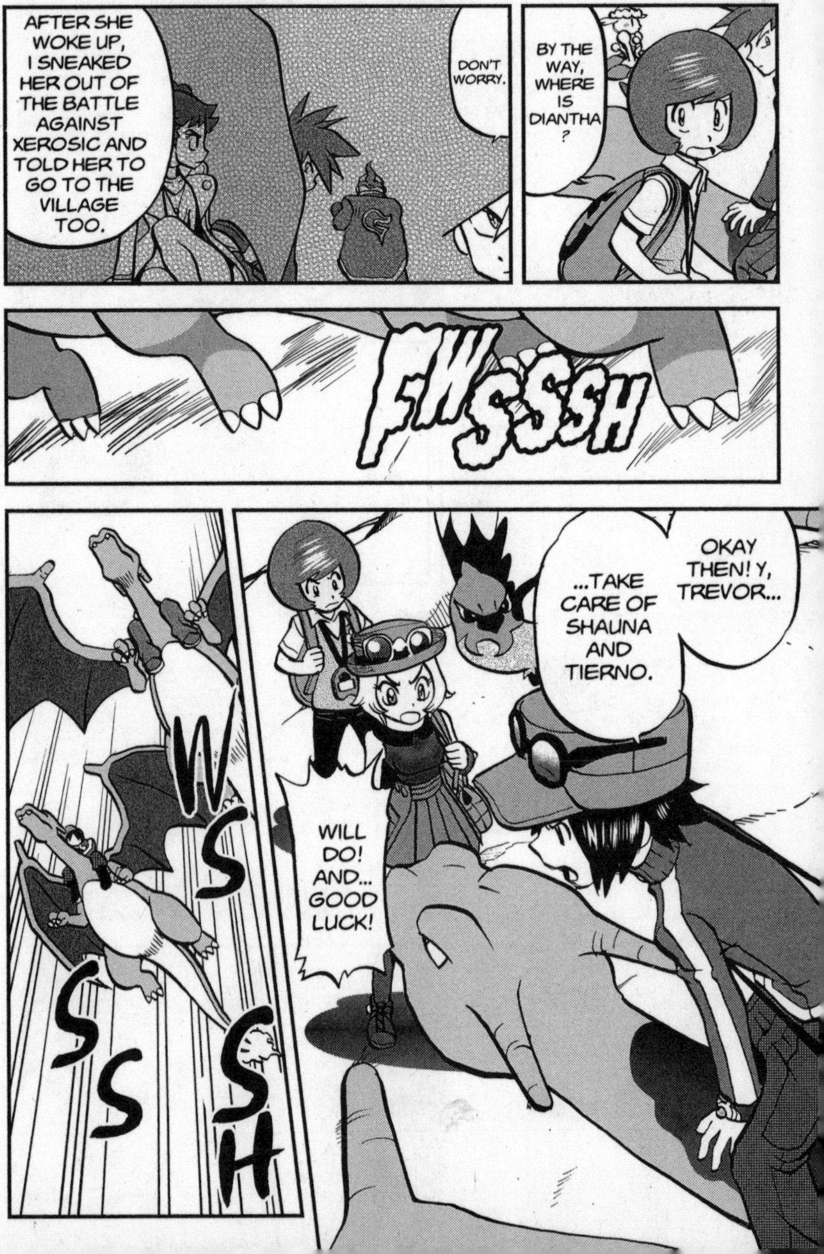
BY THE WAY, WHERE IS DIANTHA?
DON'T WORRY.
AFTER SHE WOKE UP, I SNEAKED HER OUT OF THE BATTLE AGAINST XEROSIC AND TOLD HER TO GO TO THE VILLAGE TOO.
FWSSSH
OKAY THEN! Y, TREVOR...
...TAKE CARE OF SHAUNA AND TIERNO.
WILL DO! AND... GOOD LUCK!
WSSSSH

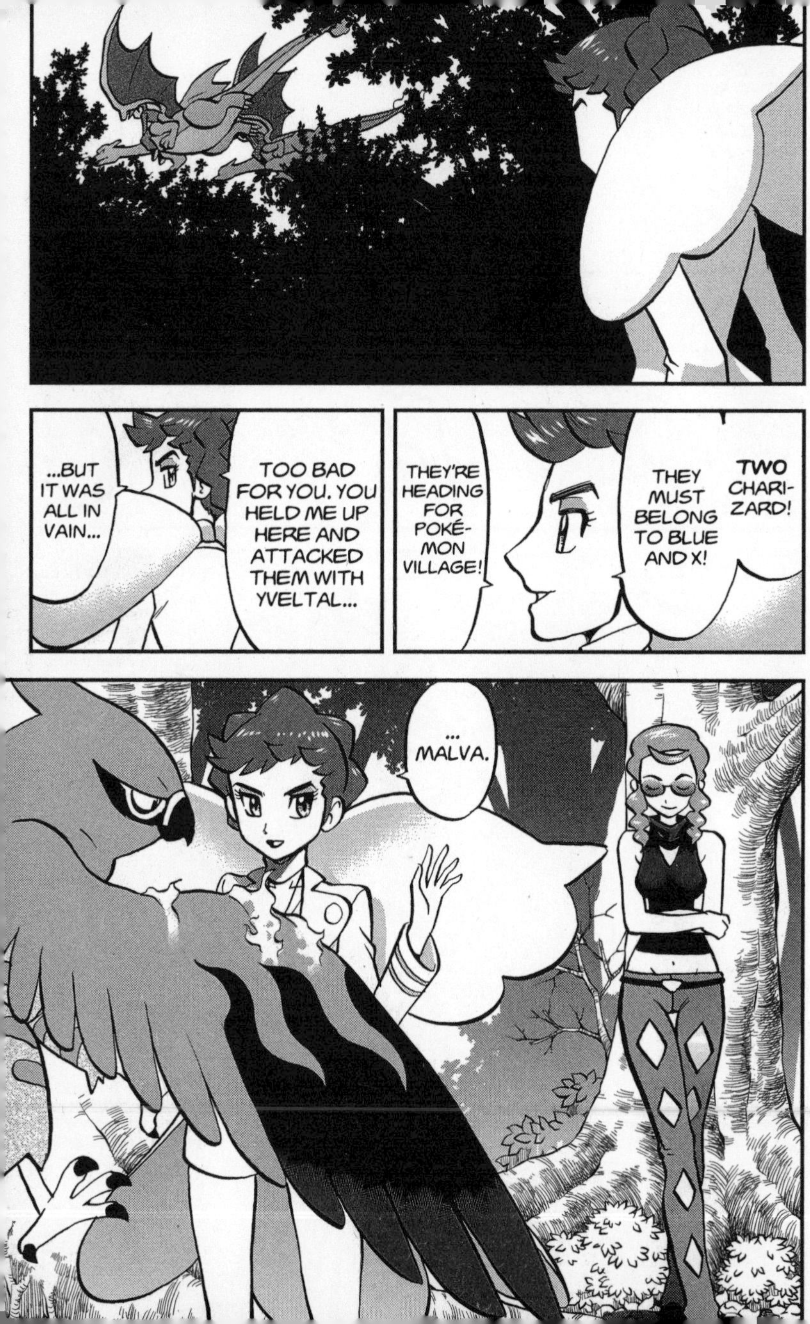
TWO CHARIZARD!
THEY MUST BELONG TO BLUE AND X!
THEY'RE HEADING FOR POKÉMON VILLAGE!
TOO BAD FOR YOU. YOU HELD ME UP HERE AND ATTACKED THEM WITH YVELTAL...
...BUT IT WAS ALL IN VAIN...
... MALVA.

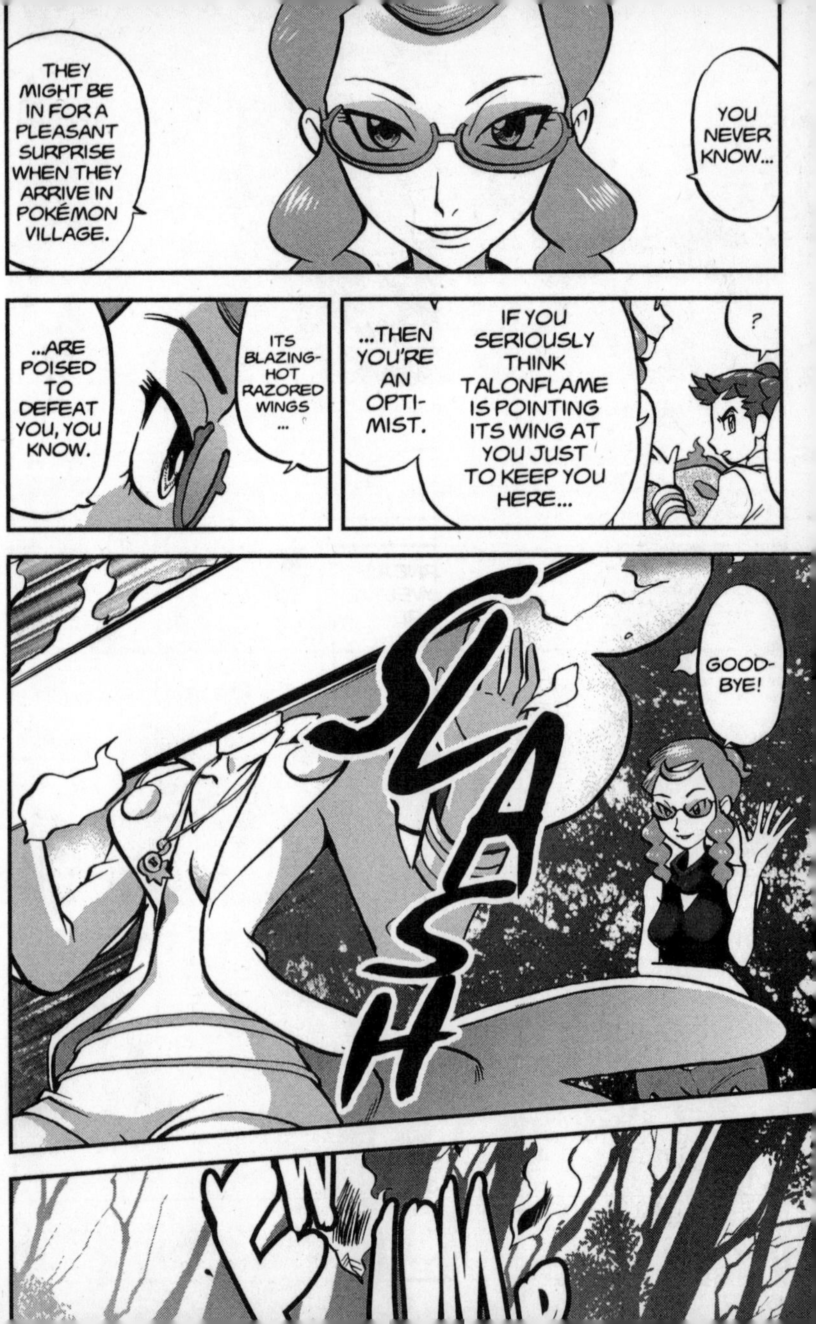
YOU NEVER KNOW...
THEY MIGHT BE IN FOR A PLEASANT SURPRISE WHEN THEY ARRIVE IN POKÉMON VILLAGE.
?
IF YOU SERIOUSLY THINK TALONFLAME IS POINTING ITS WING AT YOU JUST TO KEEP YOU HERE...
...THEN YOU'RE AN OPTI-MIST.
ITS BLAZING-HOT RAZORED WINGS...
...ARE POISED TO DEFEAT YOU, YOU KNOW.
GOOD-BYE!
SLASH

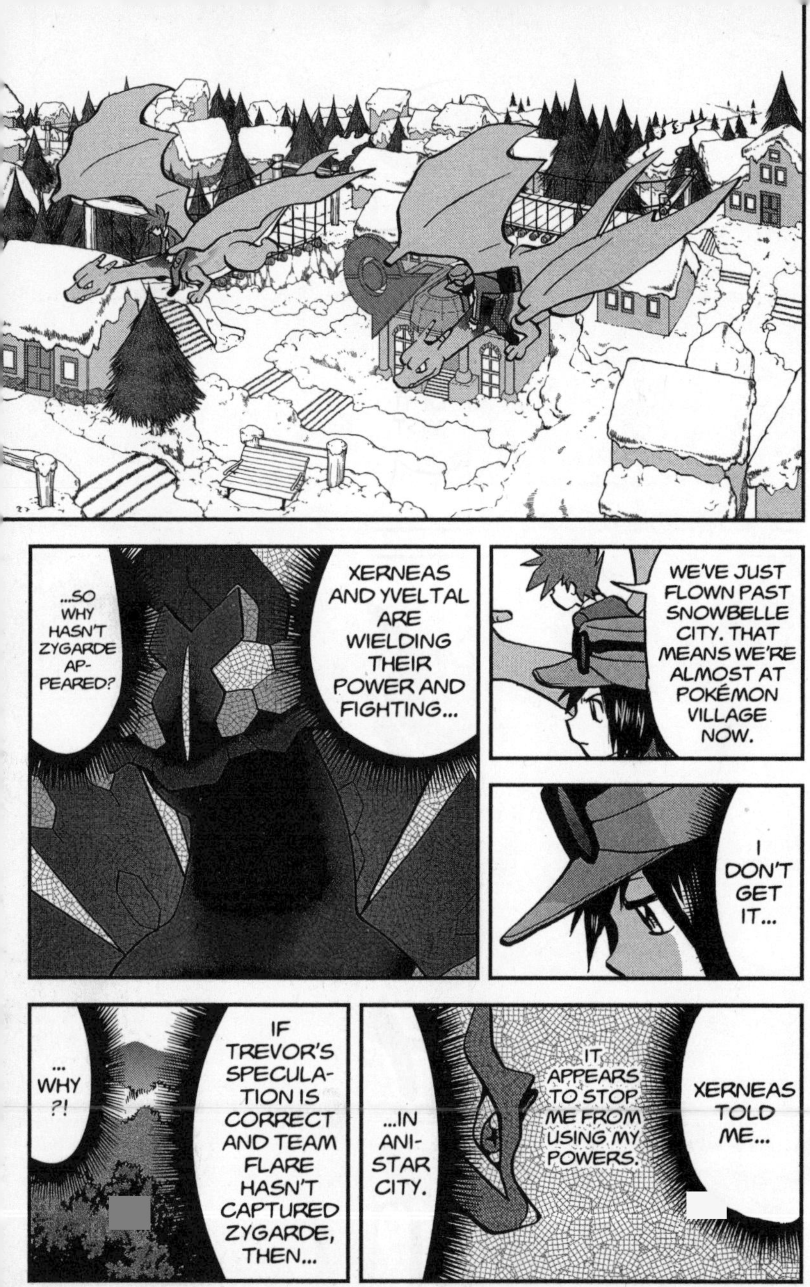
WE'VE JUST FLOWN PAST SNOWBELLE CITY. THAT MEANS WE'RE ALMOST AT POKÉMON VILLAGE NOW.
I DON'T GET IT...
XERNEAS AND YVELTAL ARE WIELDING THEIR POWER AND FIGHTING...
...SO WHY HASN'T ZYGARDE AP-PEARED?
XERNEAS TOLD ME...
IT APPEARS TO STOP ME FROM USING MY POWERS.
...IN ANI-STAR CITY.
IF TREVOR'S SPECULA-TION IS CORRECT AND TEAM FLARE HASN'T CAPTURED ZYGARDE, THEN...
...WHY ?!

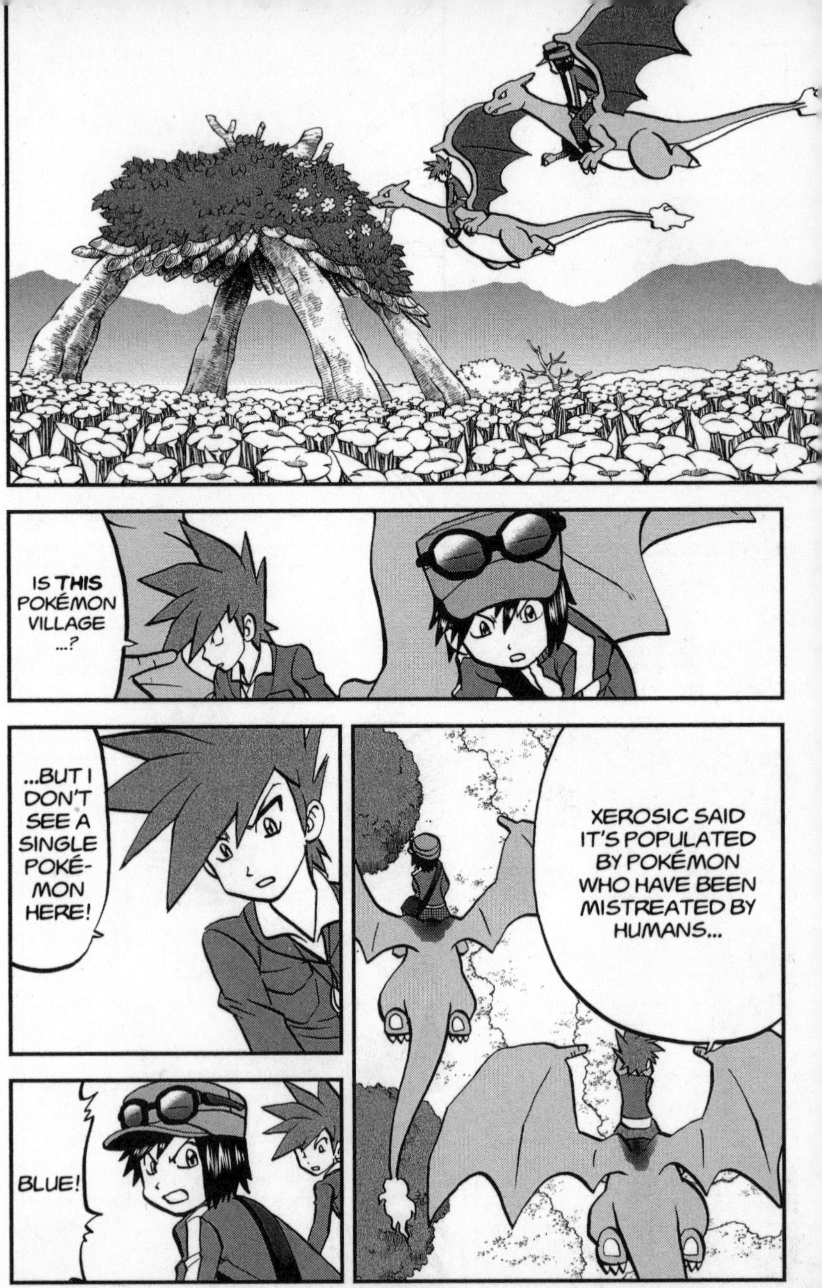
IS THIS POKÉMON VILLAGE ...?
XEROSIC SAID IT'S POPULATED BY POKÉMON WHO HAVE BEEN MISTREATED BY HUMANS...
...BUT I DON'T SEE A SINGLE POKÉ-MON HERE!
BLUE!

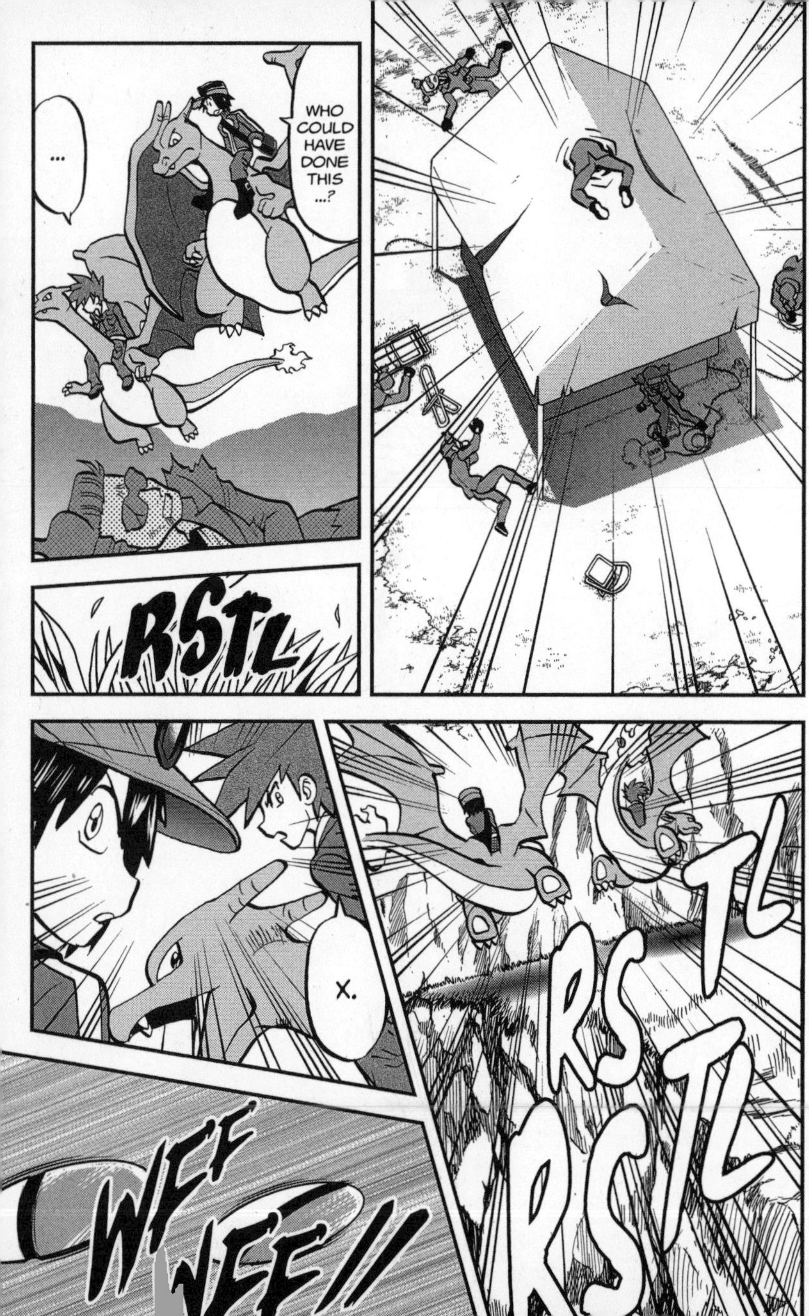
WHO COULD HAVE DONE THIS ...?
...
RSTL
RSTL
RSTL
X.
WFF WFF!!

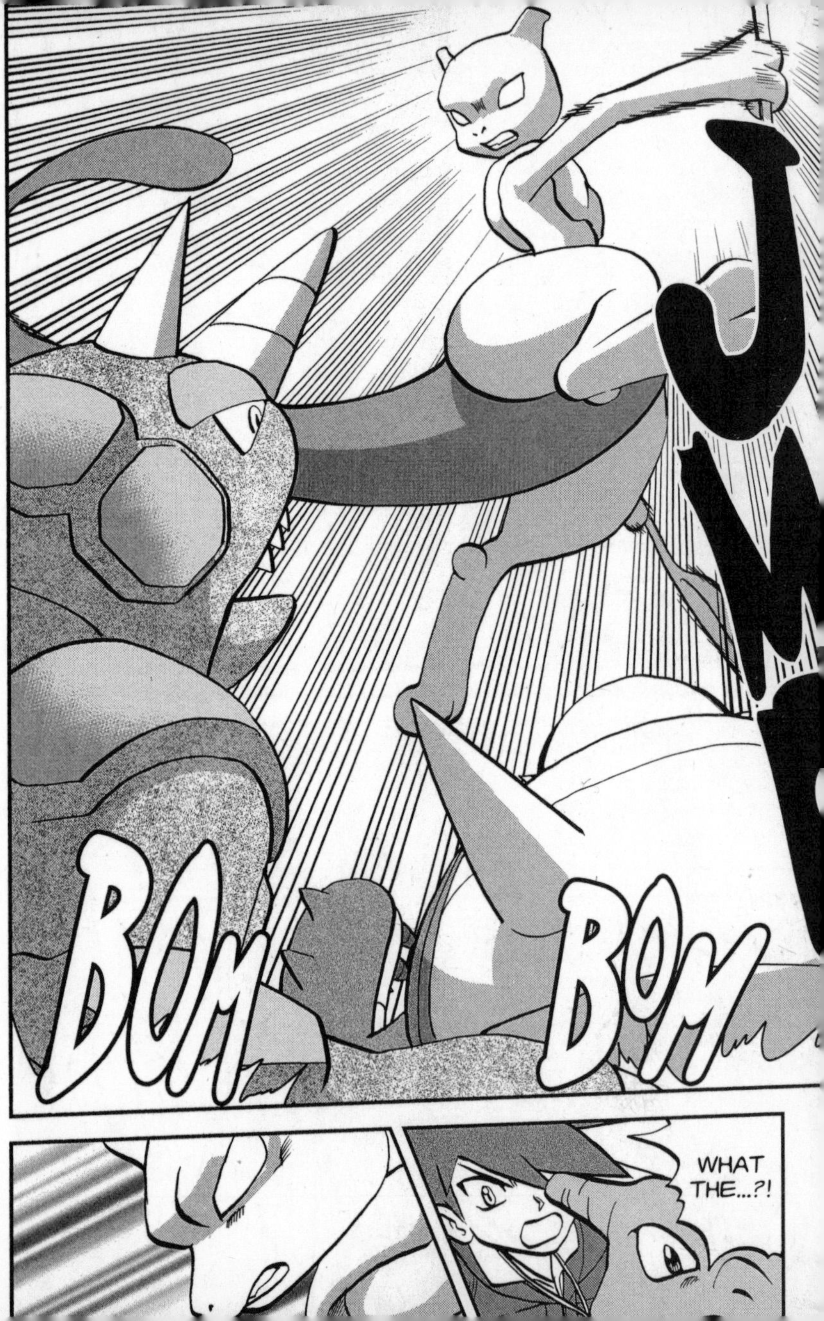
BOM
BOM
WHAT THE...?!

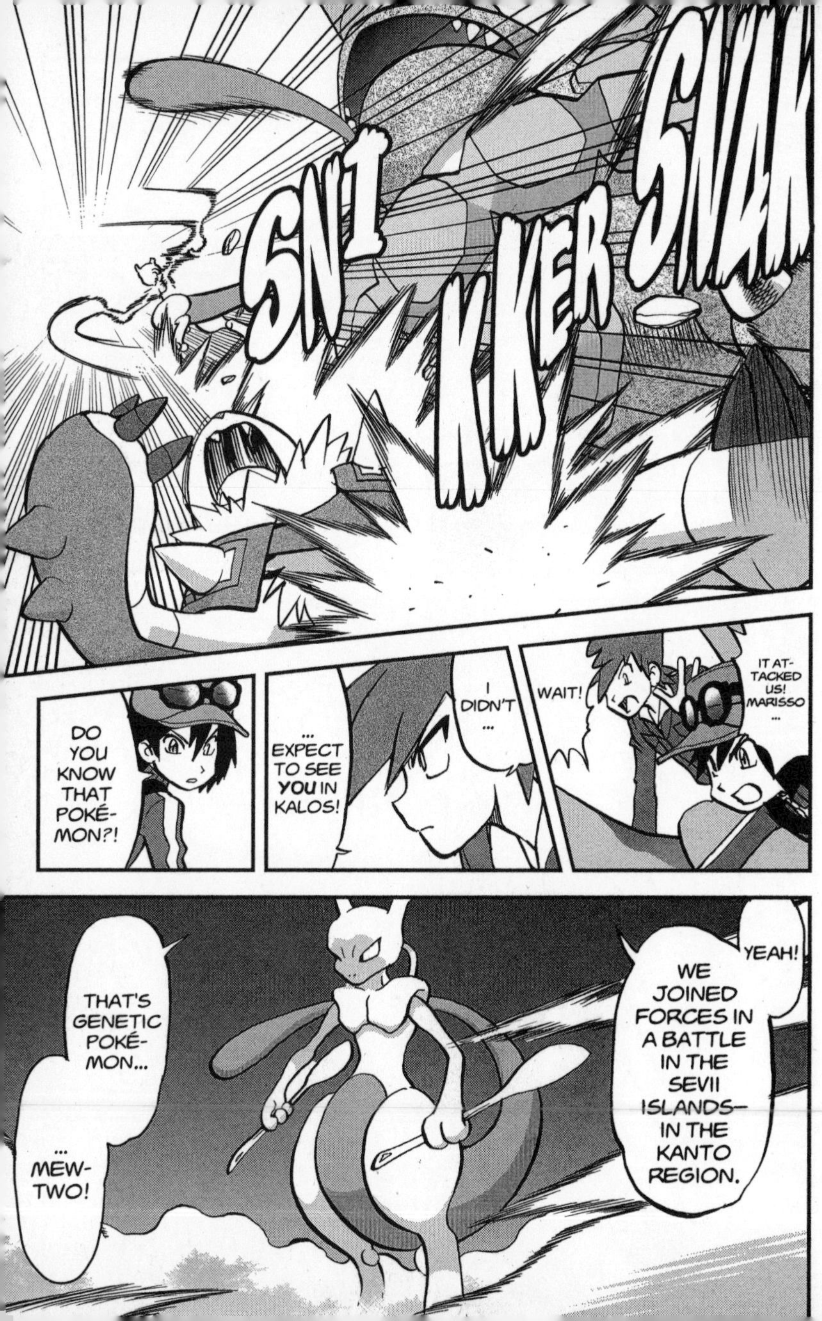
SNI
KKER
SNAK
IT ATTACKED US! MARISSO...
WAIT!
I DIDN'T...
...EXPECT TO SEE **YOU** IN KALOS!
DO YOU KNOW THAT POKÉMON?!
YEAH!
WE JOINED FORCES IN A BATTLE IN THE SEVII ISLANDS—IN THE KANTO REGION.
THAT'S GENETIC POKÉMON...
...MEWTWO!

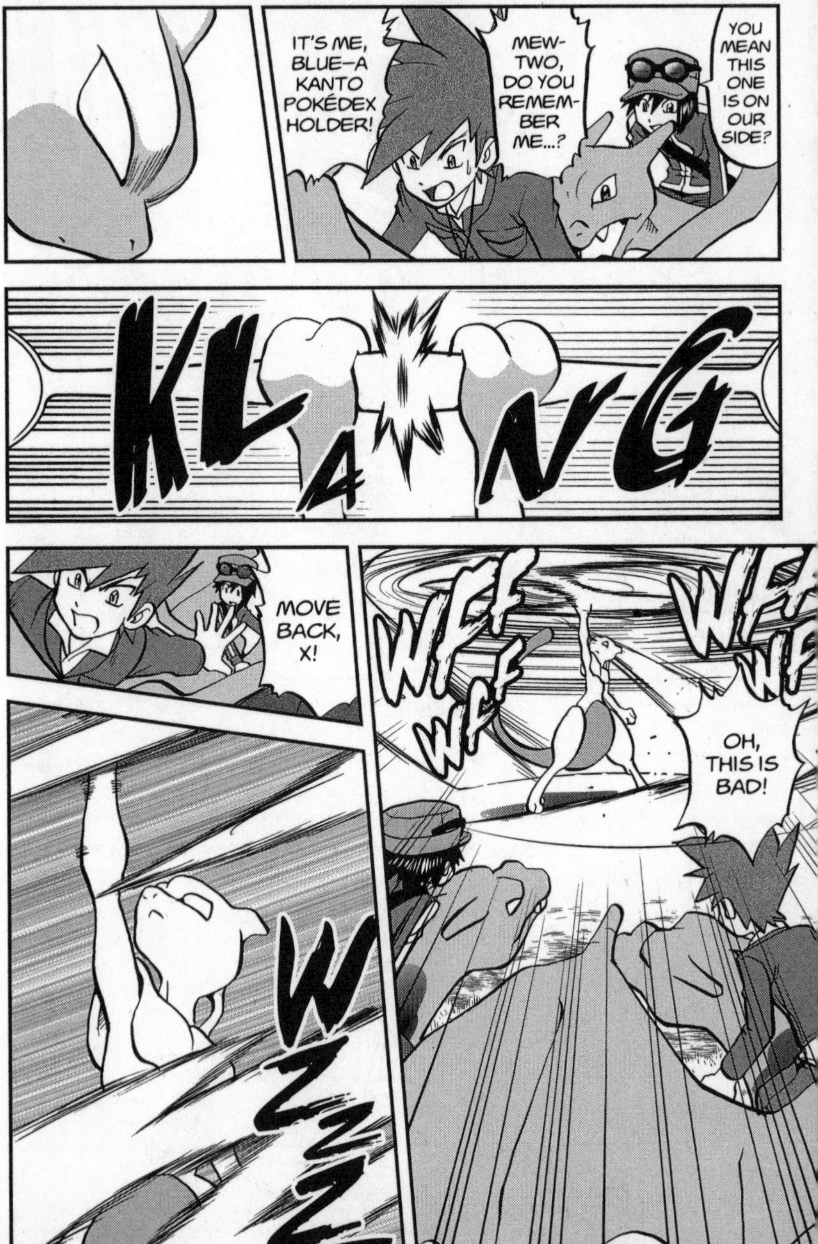

YOU MEAN THIS ONE IS ON OUR SIDE?
MEW-TWO, DO YOU REMEMBER ME...?
IT'S ME, BLUE—A KANTO POKÉDEX HOLDER!
KLANG
WFF
WFF
WFF
WFF
OH, THIS IS BAD!
MOVE BACK, X!
WZZZ

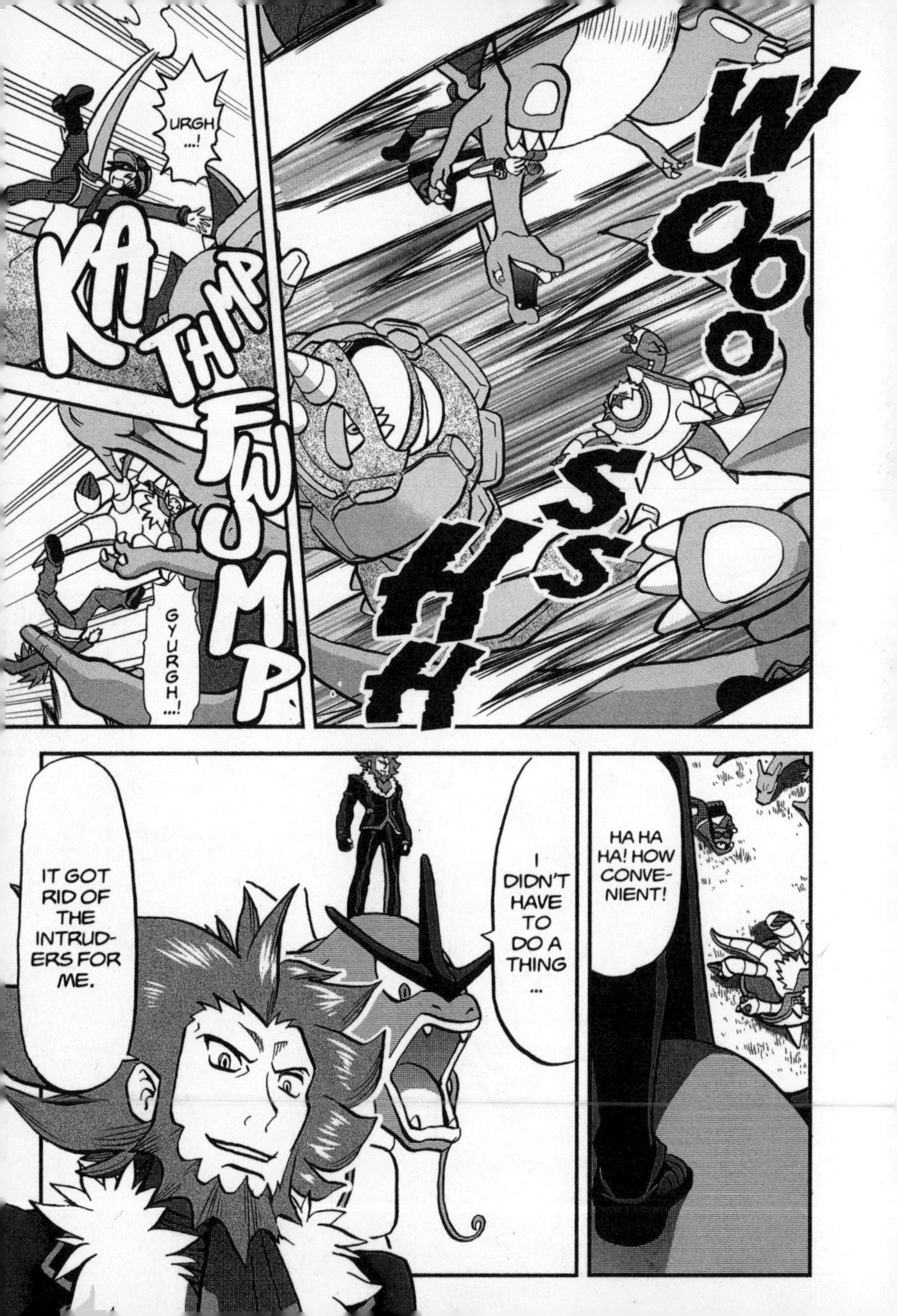
WOOOO
SSHH
URGH...!
KA THMP
FWUMP
GYURGH...!
HA HA HA! HOW CONVE-NIENT!
I DIDN'T HAVE TO DO A THING...
IT GOT RID OF THE INTRUDERS FOR ME.

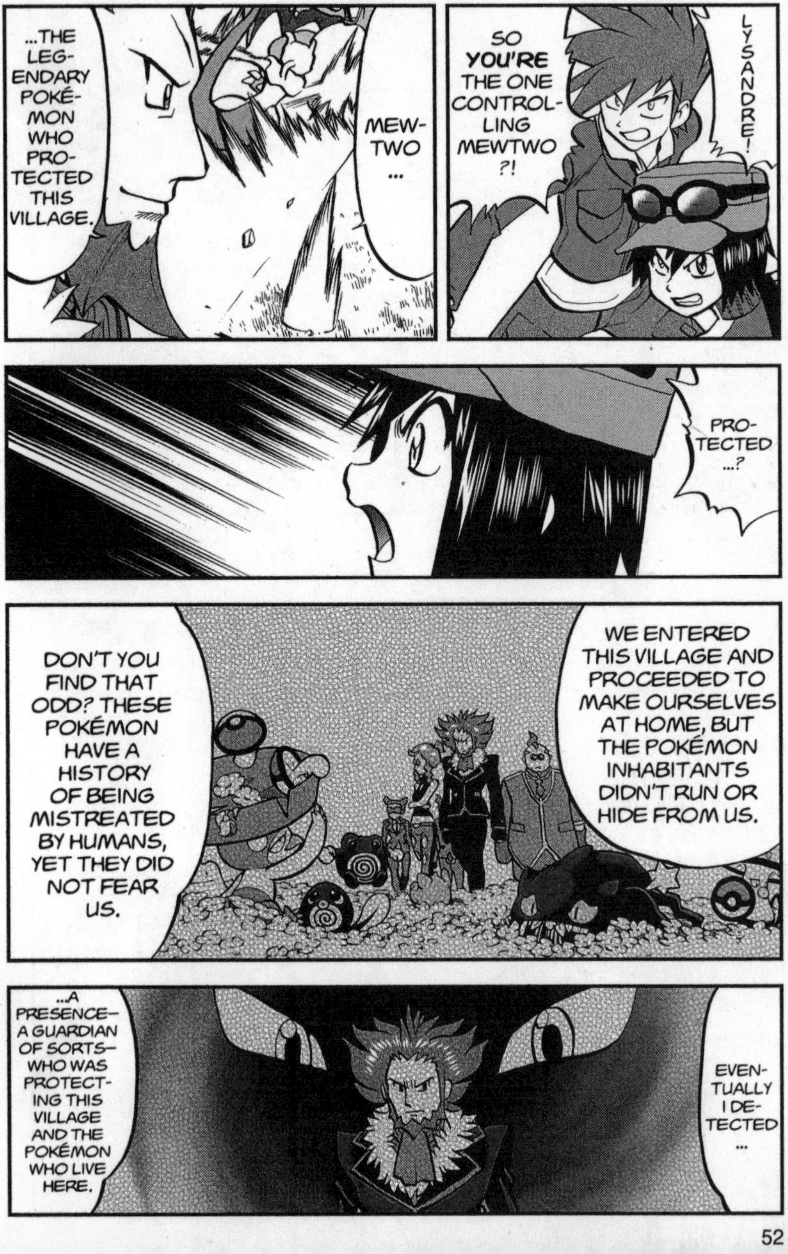
LYSANDRE!
SO **YOU'RE** THE ONE CONTROLLING MEWTWO?!
MEWTWO...
...THE LEGENDARY POKÉMON WHO PROTECTED THIS VILLAGE.
PROTECTED...?
WE ENTERED THIS VILLAGE AND PROCEEDED TO MAKE OURSELVES AT HOME, BUT THE POKÉMON INHABITANTS DIDN'T RUN OR HIDE FROM US.
DON'T YOU FIND THAT ODD? THESE POKÉMON HAVE A HISTORY OF BEING MISTREATED BY HUMANS, YET THEY DID NOT FEAR US.
EVENTUALLY I DETECTED...
...A PRESENCE—A GUARDIAN OF SORTS—WHO WAS PROTECTING THIS VILLAGE AND THE POKÉMON WHO LIVE HERE.

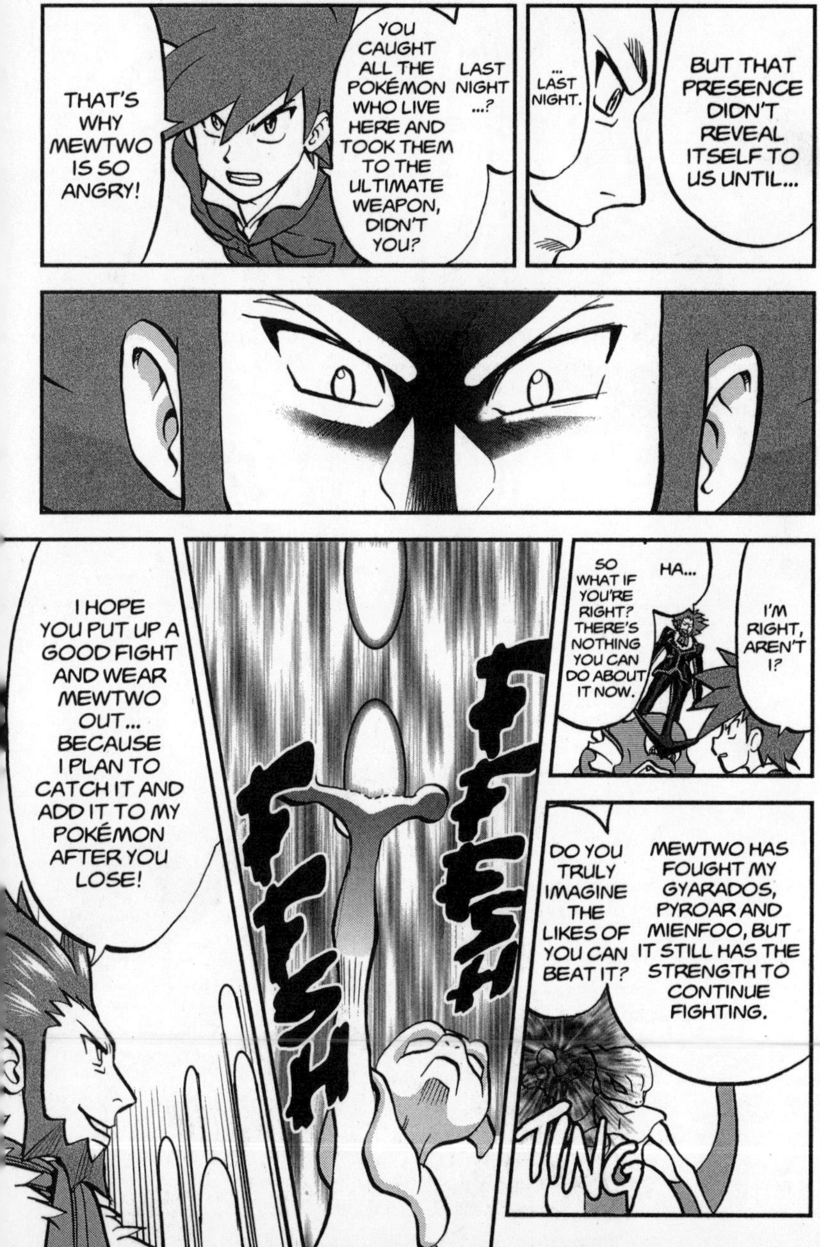
BUT THAT PRESENCE DIDN'T REVEAL ITSELF TO US UNTIL...
... LAST NIGHT.
LAST NIGHT ...?
YOU CAUGHT ALL THE POKÉMON WHO LIVE HERE AND TOOK THEM TO THE ULTIMATE WEAPON, DIDN'T YOU?
THAT'S WHY MEWTWO IS SO ANGRY!
I'M RIGHT, AREN'T I?
HA...
SO WHAT IF YOU'RE RIGHT? THERE'S NOTHING YOU CAN DO ABOUT IT NOW.
MEWTWO HAS FOUGHT MY GYARADOS, PYROAR AND MIENFOO, BUT IT STILL HAS THE STRENGTH TO CONTINUE FIGHTING.
DO YOU TRULY IMAGINE THE LIKES OF YOU CAN BEAT IT?
TING
FESH
FESH
I HOPE YOU PUT UP A GOOD FIGHT AND WEAR MEWTWO OUT... BECAUSE I PLAN TO CATCH IT AND ADD IT TO MY POKÉMON AFTER YOU LOSE!

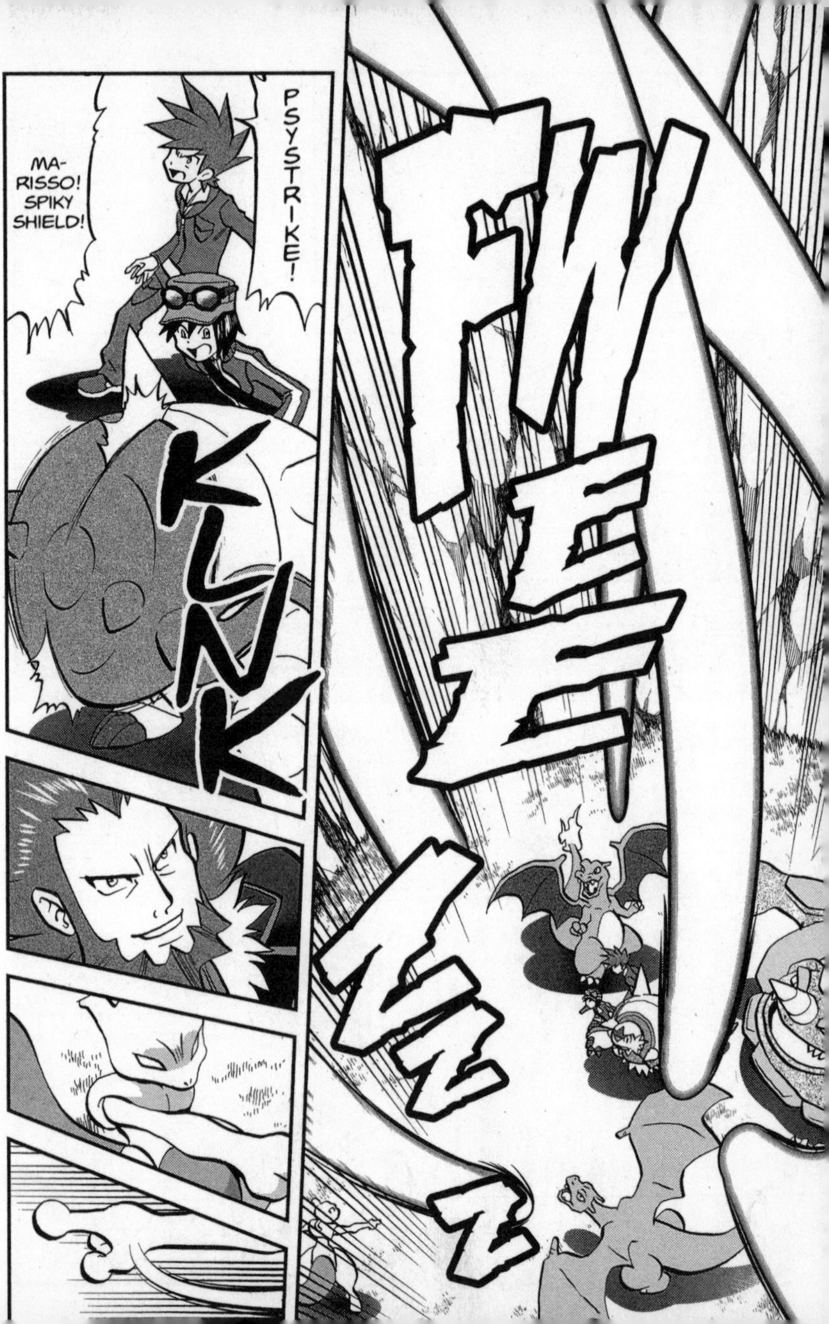
FWEEE
PSYSTRIKE!
MA-RISSO! SPIKY SHIELD!
KLNK

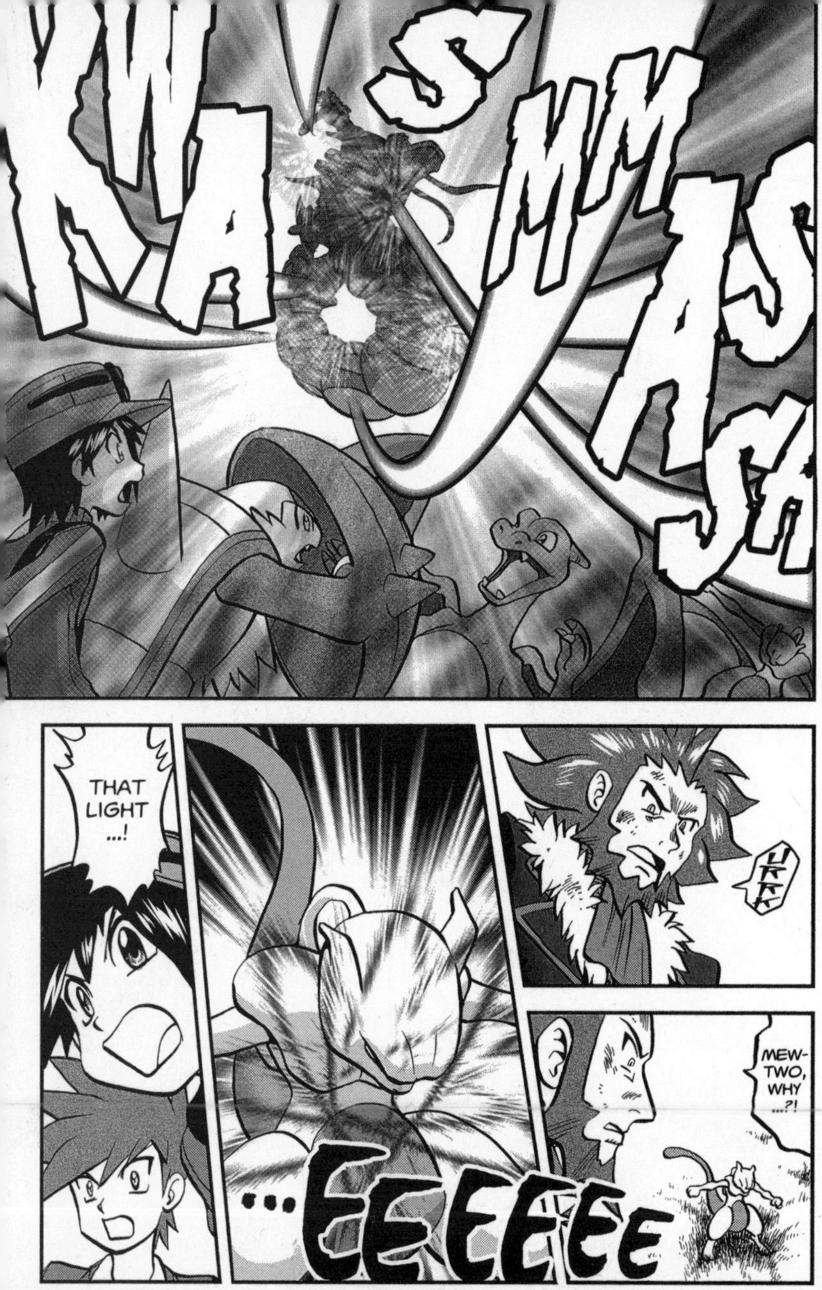
KWA
SMMAS
AS
URRK
MEW-TWO, WHY ...?!
...EEEEEE
THAT LIGHT ...!

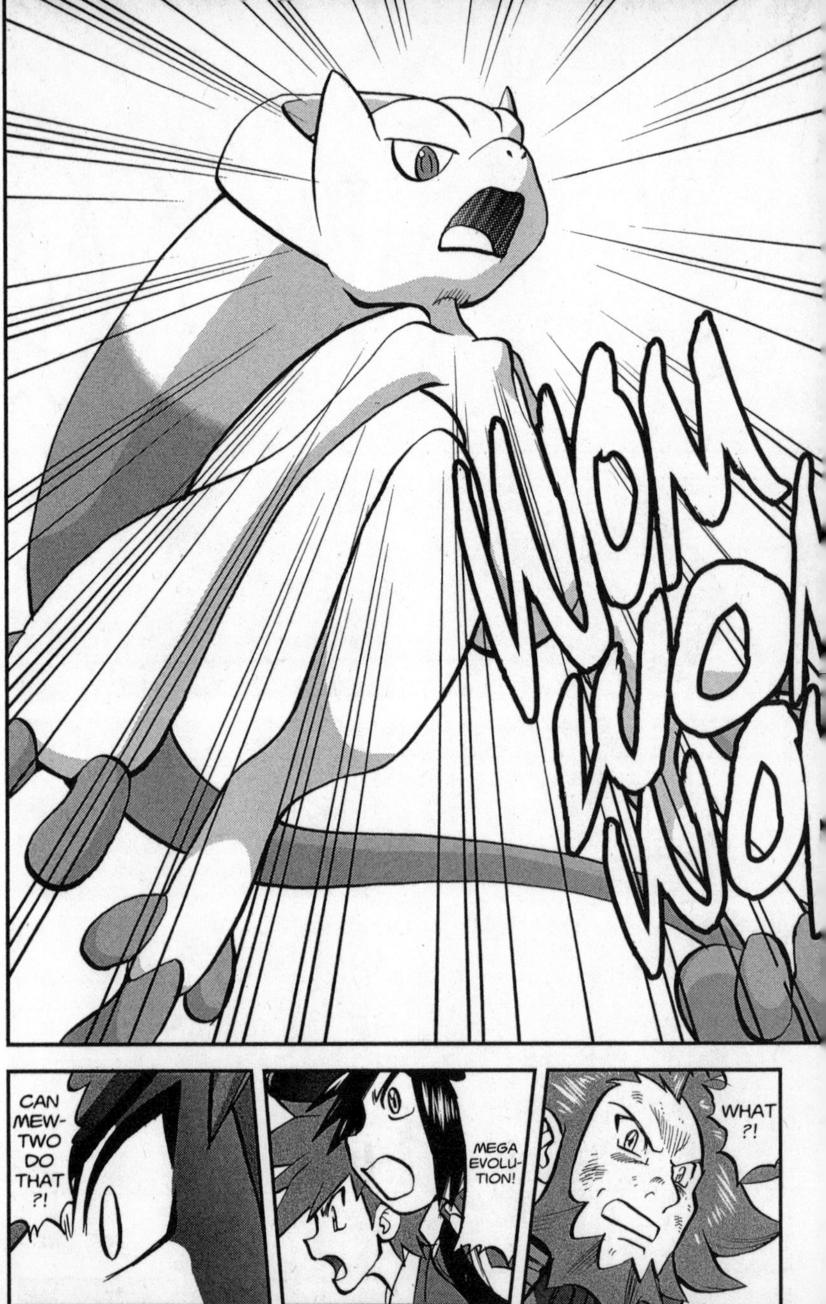
WUOM
WHAT?!
MEGA EVOLUTION!
CAN MEWTWO DO THAT?!

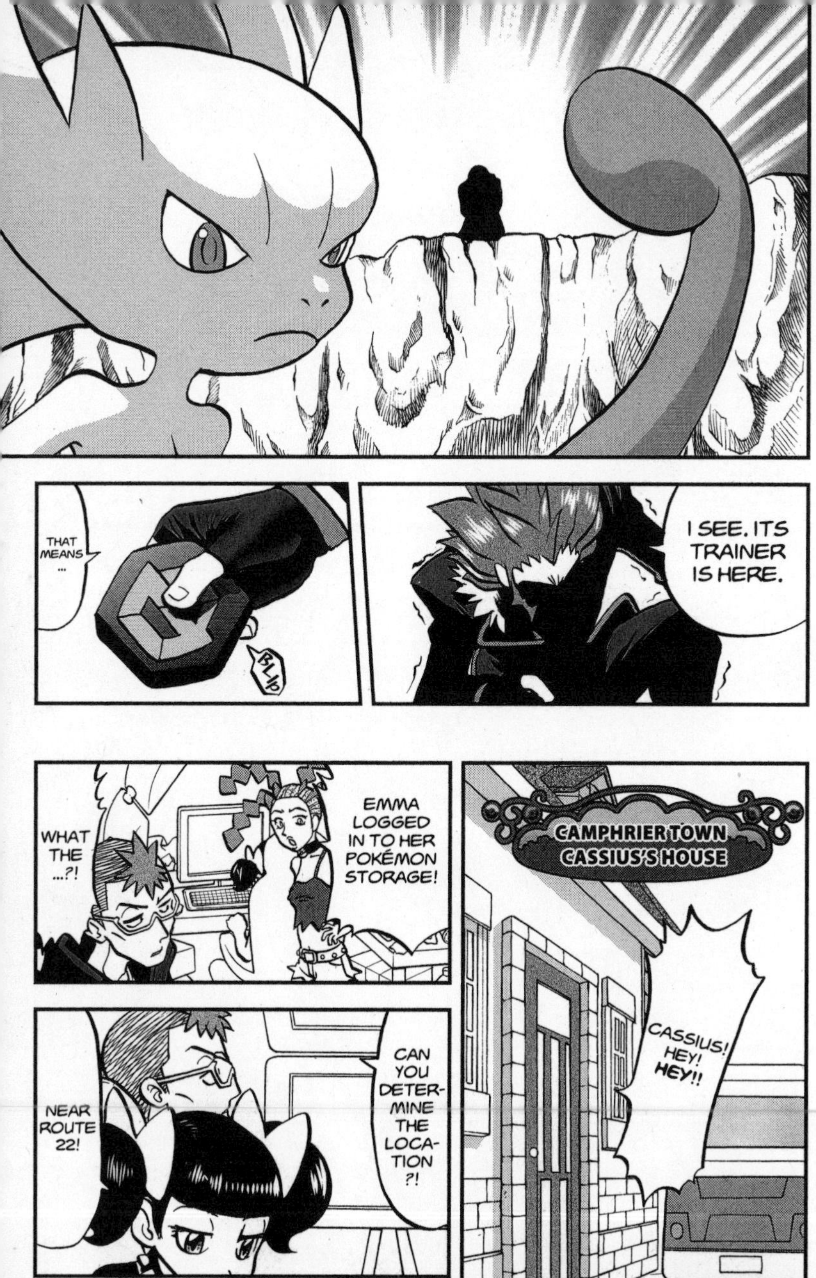

I SEE. ITS TRAINER IS HERE.
THAT MEANS ...
BLIP
CAMPHRIER TOWN
CASSIUS'S HOUSE
CASSIUS! HEY! HEY!!
EMMA LOGGED IN TO HER POKÉMON STORAGE!
WHAT THE ...?!
CAN YOU DETERMINE THE LOCATION?!
NEAR ROUTE 22!

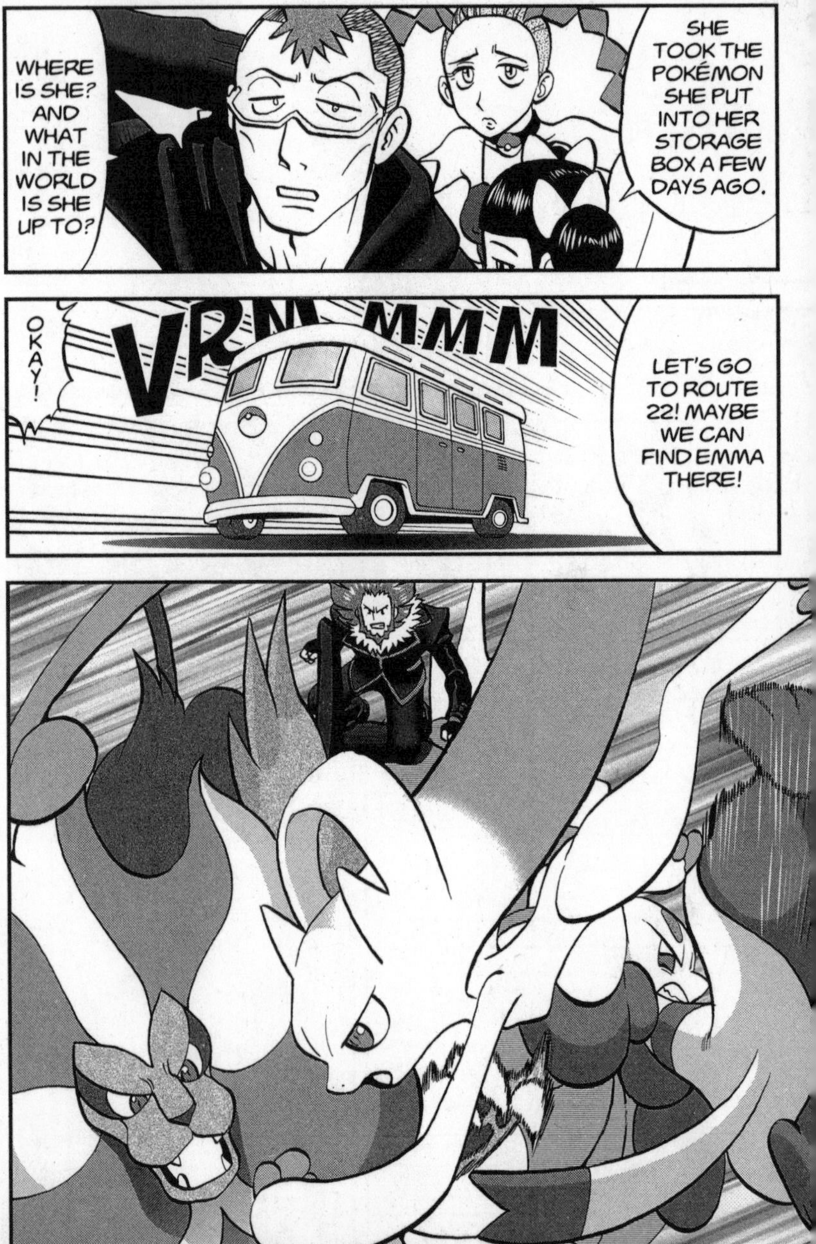
SHE TOOK THE POKÉMON SHE PUT INTO HER STORAGE BOX A FEW DAYS AGO.
WHERE IS SHE? AND WHAT IN THE WORLD IS SHE UP TO?
LET'S GO TO ROUTE 22! MAYBE WE CAN FIND EMMA THERE!
VRMMMMM
OKAY!

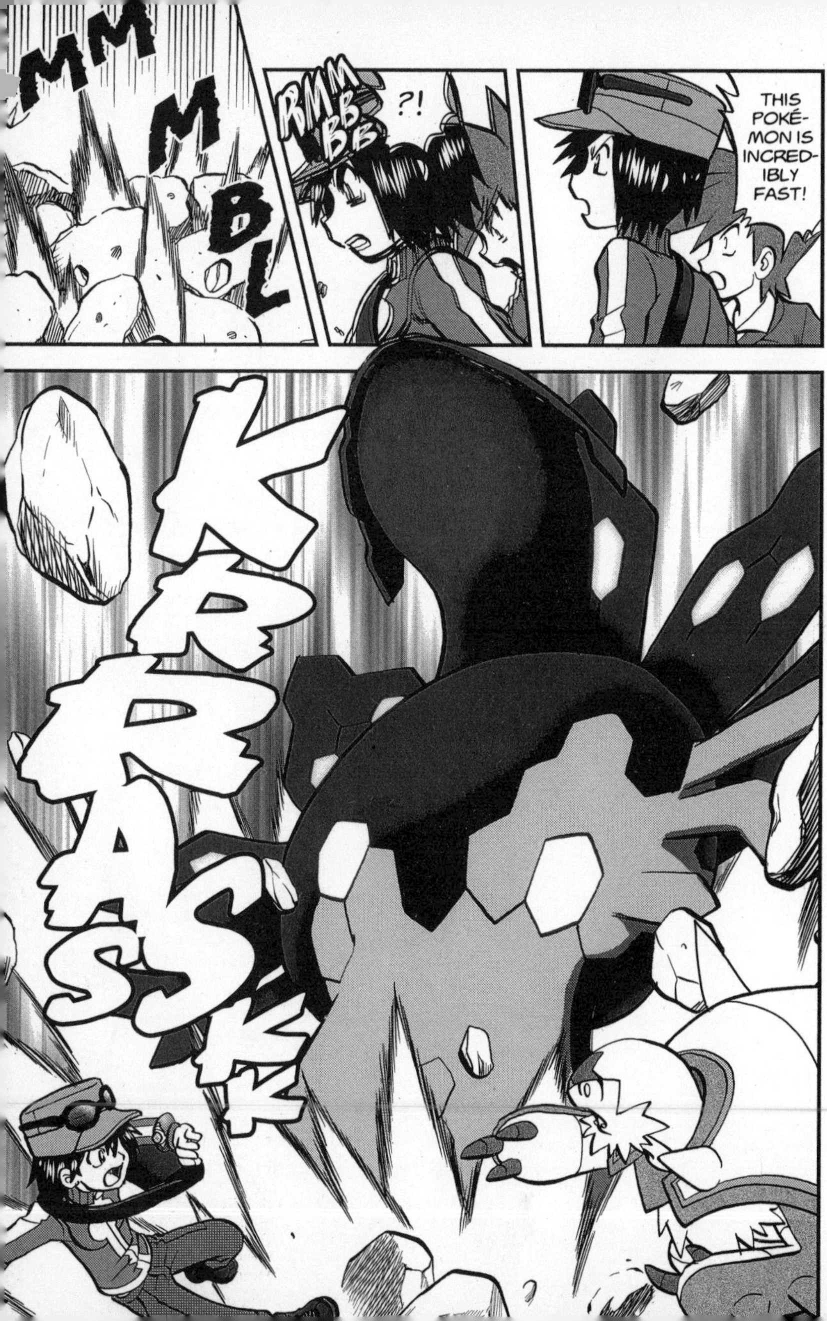
THIS POKÉ-MON IS INCRED-IBLY FAST!
RMMBBB
?!
MMMBL
KRRASSKK

Current Location

Route 18
Vallée Étroite Way

This path is best known for its trolley, once used for the coal mine, and the curious Inverse Battle House.

▼

Couriway Town

The railway brings people from great distances to see the huge, majestic falls.

▼

Route 19
Grande Vallée Way

This great valley can now be crossed thanks to its long bridge, built with the help of many Pokémon.

▼

Snowbelle City

They say the cold air flowing from the Pokémon Gym is responsible for this city's frozen state.

▼

Route 20
Winding Woods

This path was designed to disturb the woods as little as possible, so it twists and turns among the trees.

▼

Pokémon Village

Legends say a place exists where Pokémon live in hiding, but no one has ever found it.

Adventure 36 Mewtwo Angered

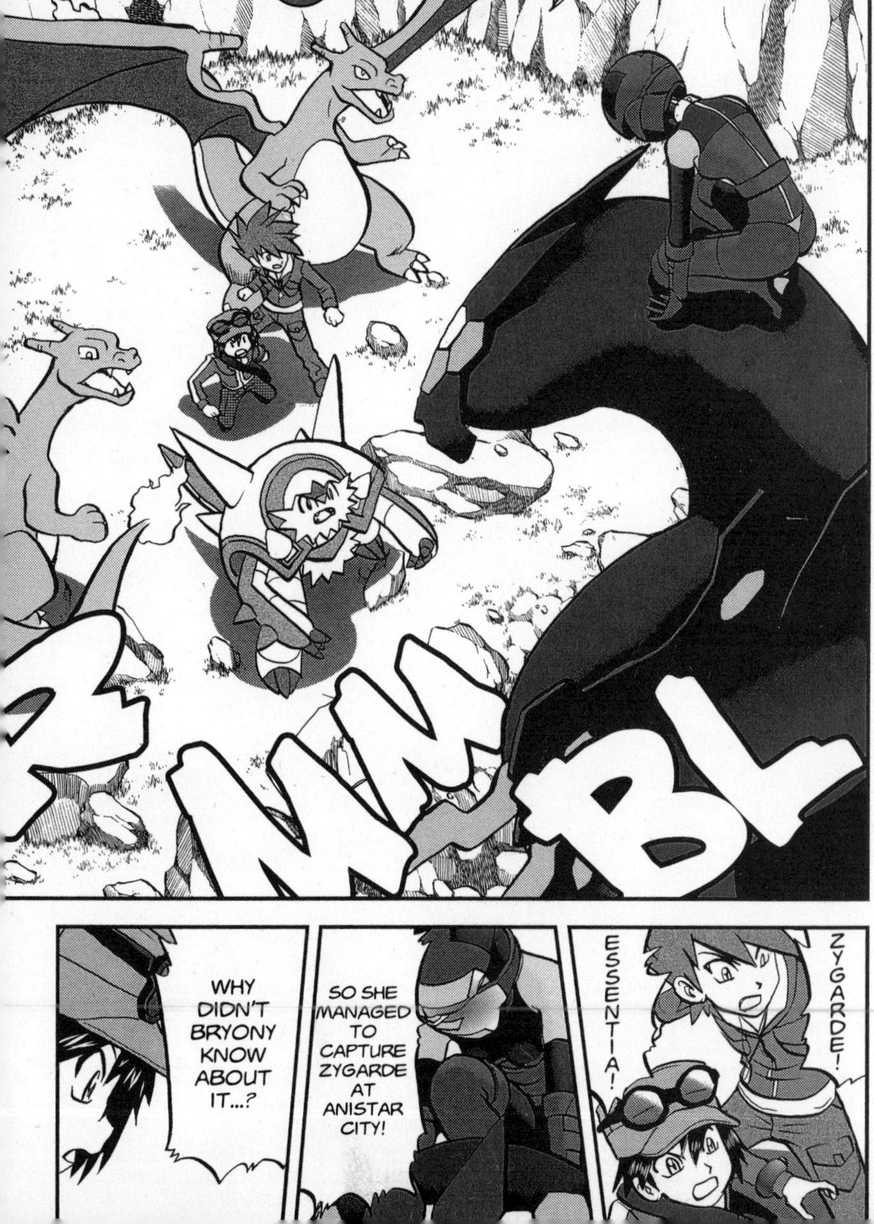
ZYGARDE!
ESSENTIA!
SO SHE MANAGED TO CAPTURE ZYGARDE AT ANISTAR CITY!
WHY DIDN'T BRYONY KNOW ABOUT IT...?

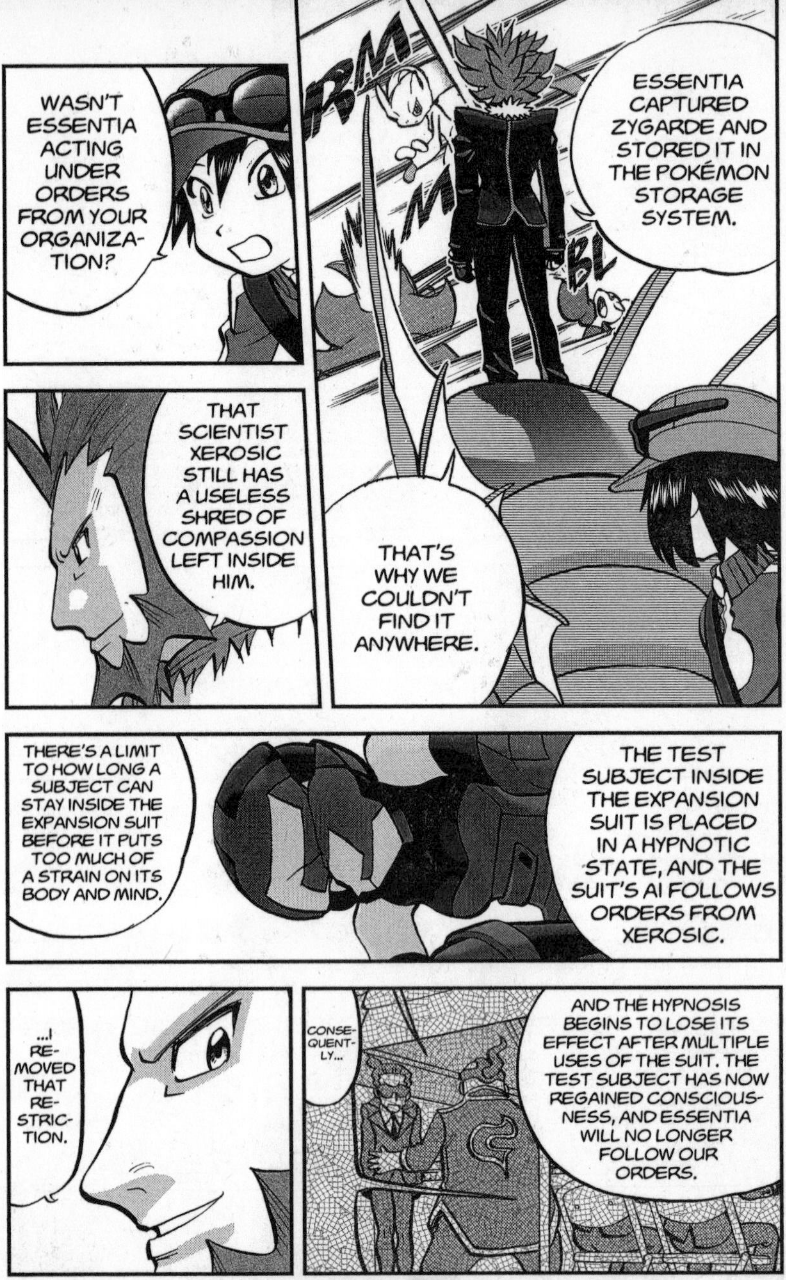
ESSENTIA CAPTURED ZYGARDE AND STORED IT IN THE POKÉMON STORAGE SYSTEM.
THAT'S WHY WE COULDN'T FIND IT ANYWHERE.
WASN'T ESSENTIA ACTING UNDER ORDERS FROM YOUR ORGANIZA-TION?
THAT SCIENTIST XEROSIC STILL HAS A USELESS SHRED OF COMPASSION LEFT INSIDE HIM.
THE TEST SUBJECT INSIDE THE EXPANSION SUIT IS PLACED IN A HYPNOTIC STATE, AND THE SUIT'S AI FOLLOWS ORDERS FROM XEROSIC.
THERE'S A LIMIT TO HOW LONG A SUBJECT CAN STAY INSIDE THE EXPANSION SUIT BEFORE IT PUTS TOO MUCH OF A STRAIN ON ITS BODY AND MIND.
AND THE HYPNOSIS BEGINS TO LOSE ITS EFFECT AFTER MULTIPLE USES OF THE SUIT. THE TEST SUBJECT HAS NOW REGAINED CONSCIOUS-NESS, AND ESSENTIA WILL NO LONGER FOLLOW OUR ORDERS.
CONSE-QUENT-LY...
...I RE-MOVED THAT RE-STRIC-TION.

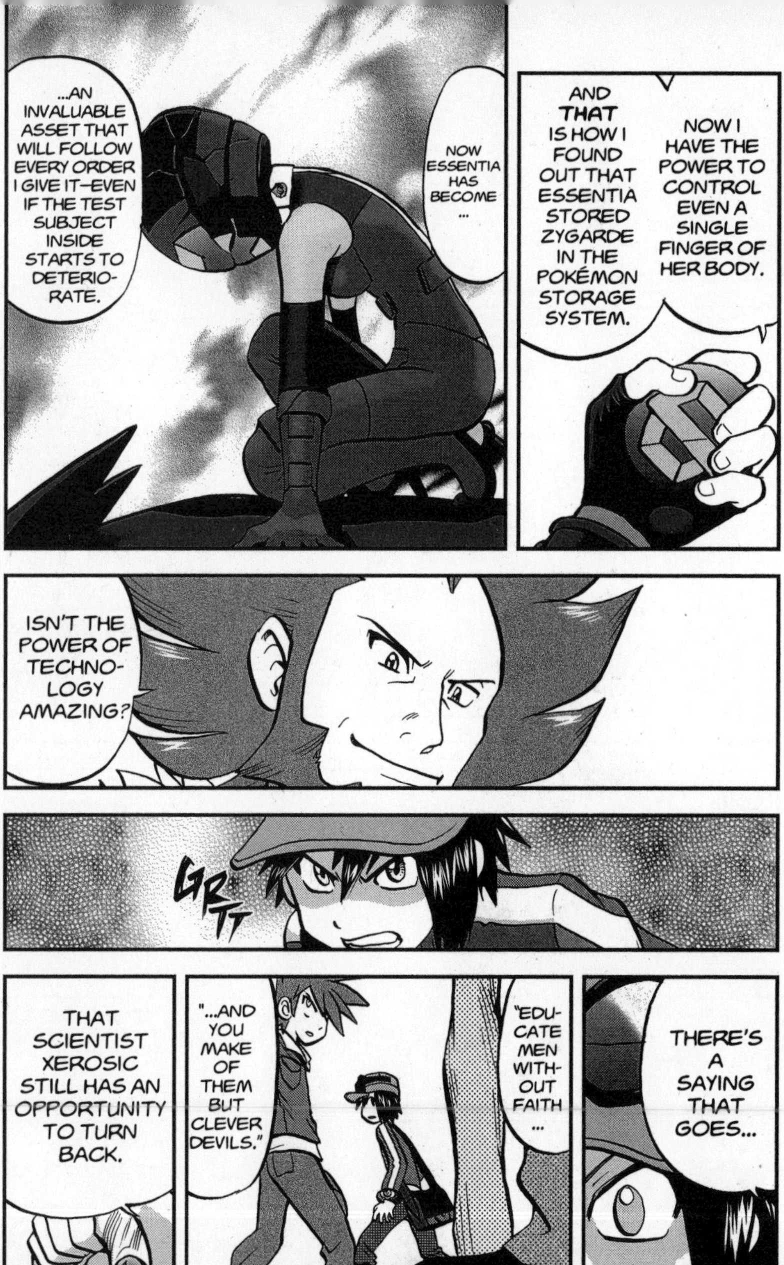
NOW I HAVE THE POWER TO CONTROL EVEN A SINGLE FINGER OF HER BODY.
AND THAT IS HOW I FOUND OUT THAT ESSENTIA STORED ZYGARDE IN THE POKÉMON STORAGE SYSTEM.
NOW ESSENTIA HAS BECOME ...
...AN INVALUABLE ASSET THAT WILL FOLLOW EVERY ORDER I GIVE IT—EVEN IF THE TEST SUBJECT INSIDE STARTS TO DETERIO-RATE.
ISN'T THE POWER OF TECHNO-LOGY AMAZING?
GRTT
THERE'S A SAYING THAT GOES...
"EDU-CATE MEN WITH-OUT FAITH ...
"...AND YOU MAKE OF THEM BUT CLEVER DEVILS."
THAT SCIENTIST XEROSIC STILL HAS AN OPPORTUNITY TO TURN BACK.

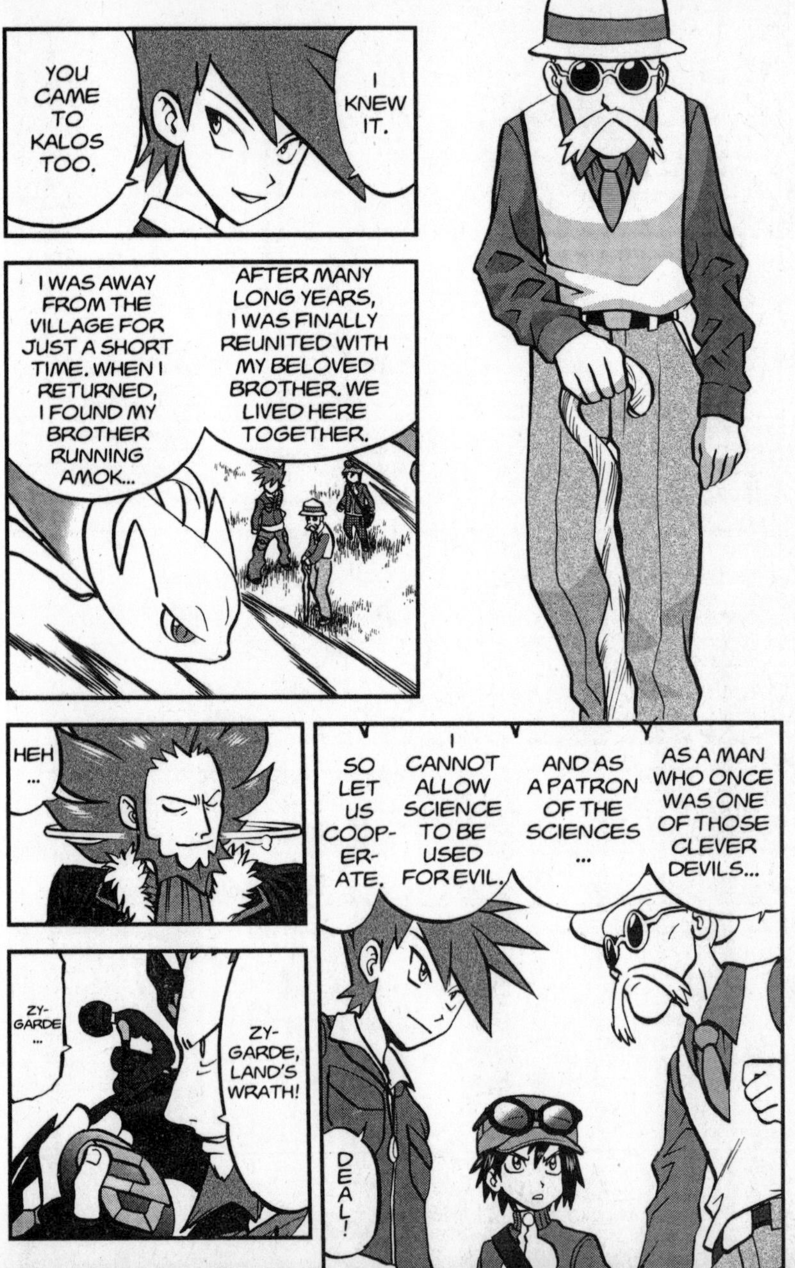
I KNEW IT.
YOU CAME TO KALOS TOO.
AFTER MANY LONG YEARS, I WAS FINALLY REUNITED WITH MY BELOVED BROTHER. WE LIVED HERE TOGETHER.
I WAS AWAY FROM THE VILLAGE FOR JUST A SHORT TIME. WHEN I RETURNED, I FOUND MY BROTHER RUNNING AMOK...
AS A MAN WHO ONCE WAS ONE OF THOSE CLEVER DEVILS...
AND AS A PATRON OF THE SCIENCES ...
I CANNOT ALLOW SCIENCE TO BE USED FOR EVIL.
SO LET US COOP-ER-ATE.
DEAL!
HEH ...
ZY-GARDE, LAND'S WRATH!
ZY-GARDE ...

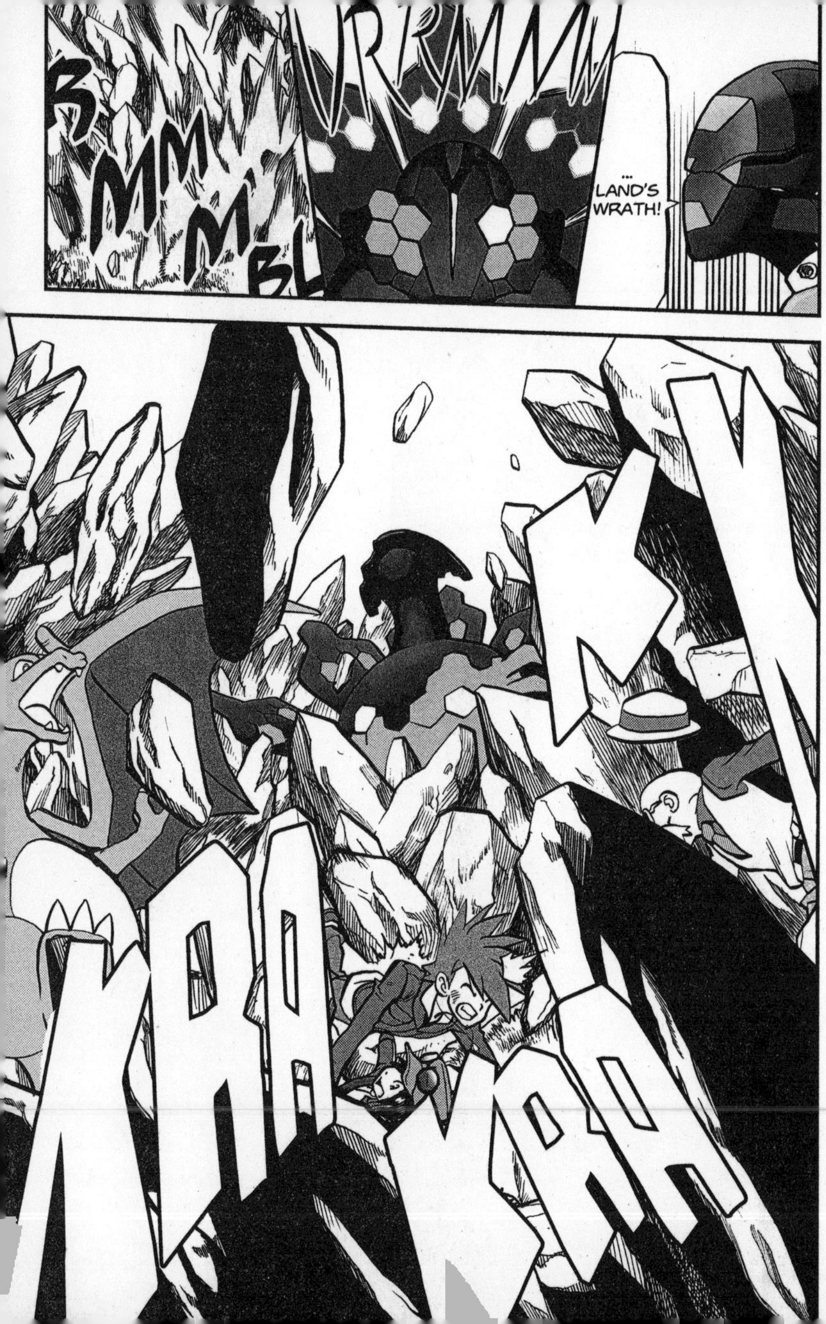
VRRMMM
... LAND'S WRATH!

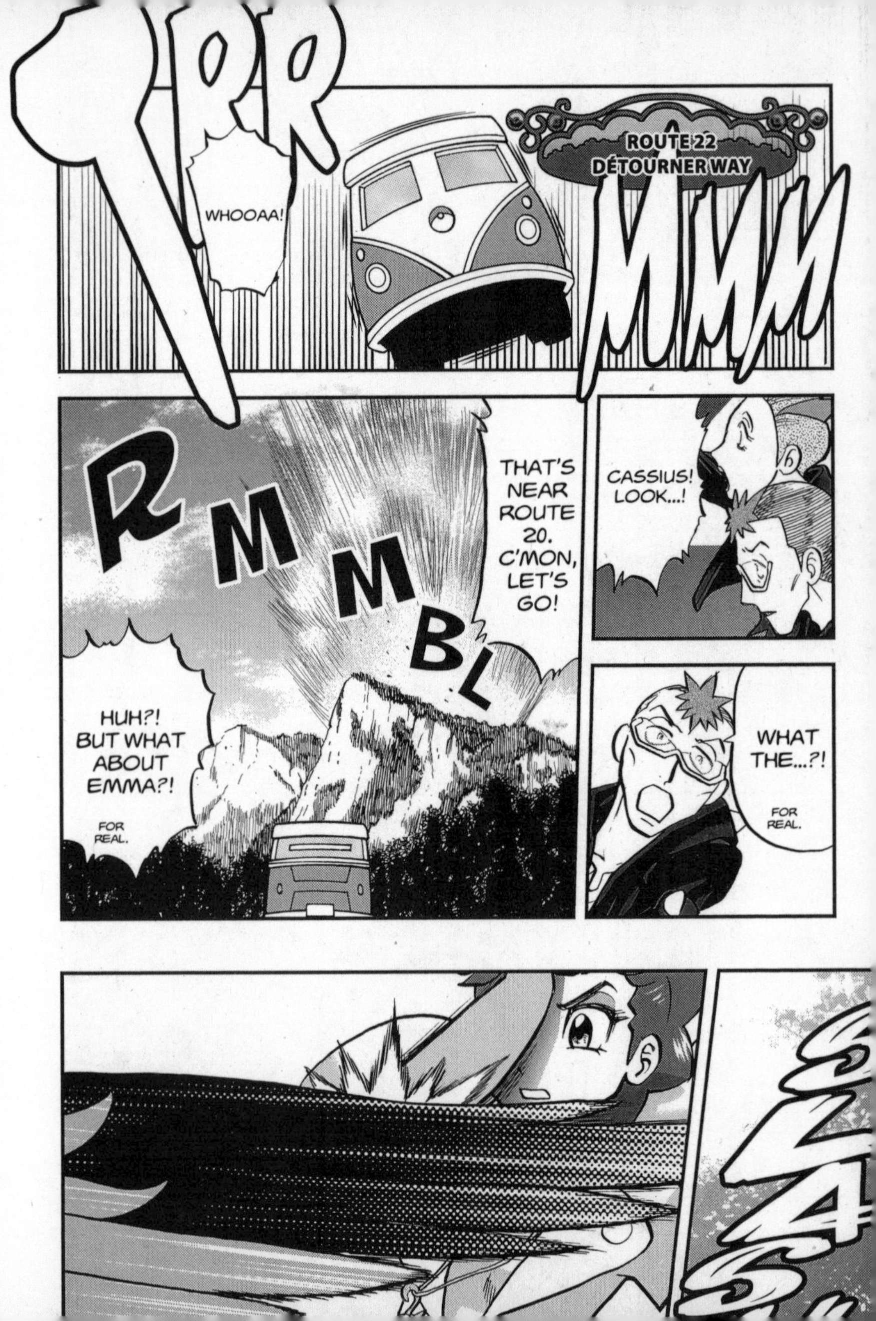
ROUTE 22
DÉTOURNER WAY
WHOOAA!
CASSIUS! LOOK...!
WHAT THE...?!
FOR REAL.
THAT'S NEAR ROUTE 20. C'MON, LET'S GO!
RMMBL
HUH?! BUT WHAT ABOUT EMMA?!
FOR REAL.

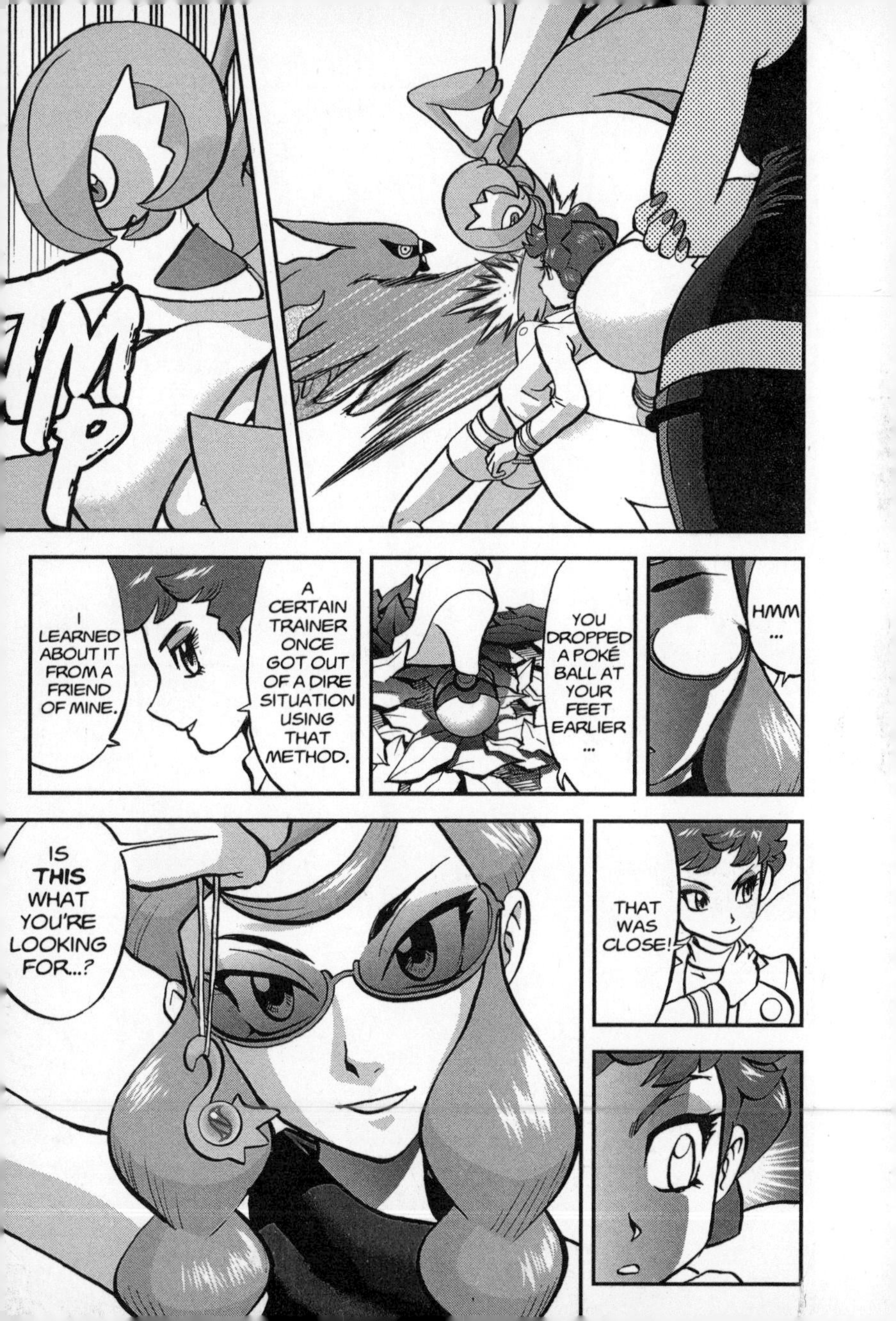
MP
HMM ...
YOU DROPPED A POKÉ BALL AT YOUR FEET EARLIER ...
A CERTAIN TRAINER ONCE GOT OUT OF A DIRE SITUATION USING THAT METHOD.
I LEARNED ABOUT IT FROM A FRIEND OF MINE.
THAT WAS CLOSE!
IS **THIS** WHAT YOU'RE LOOKING FOR...?

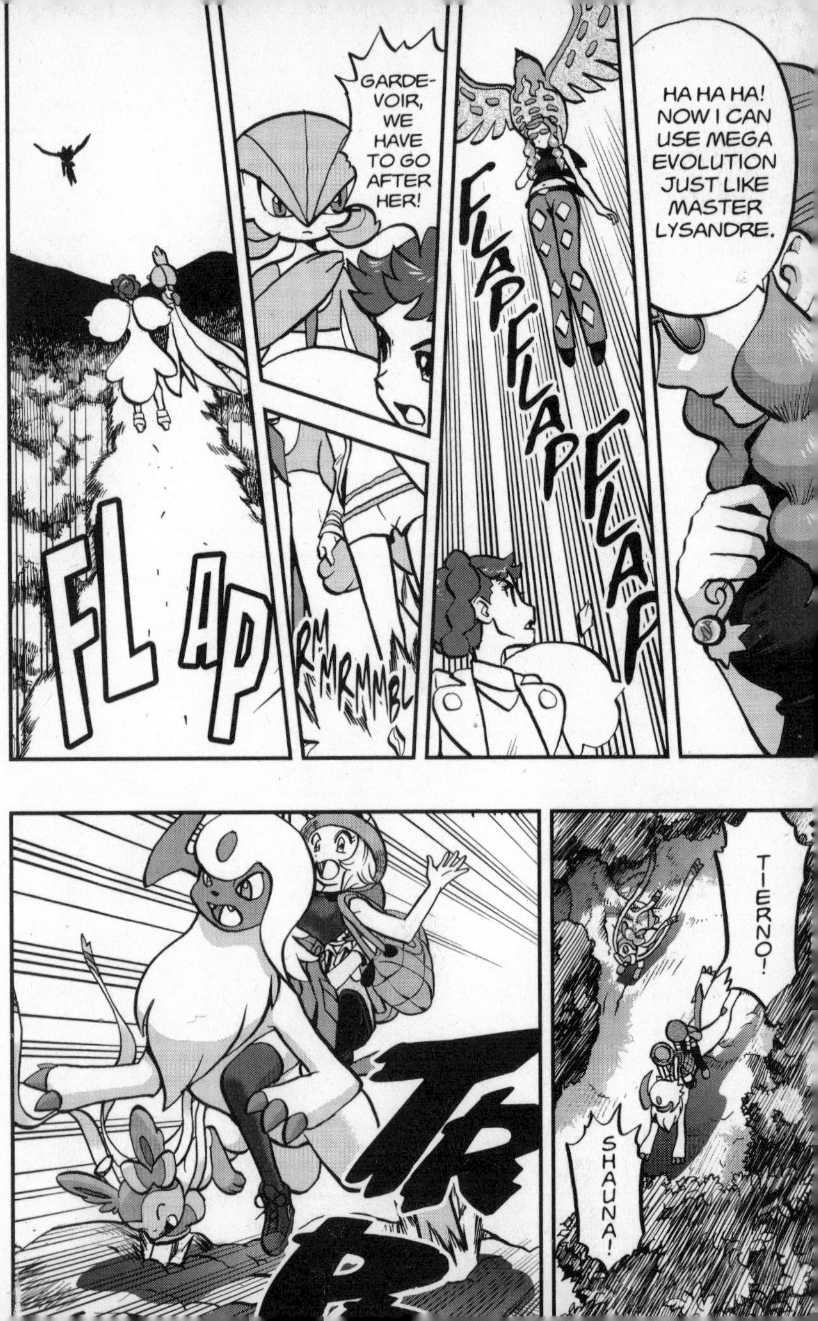
HA HA HA! NOW I CAN USE MEGA EVOLUTION JUST LIKE MASTER LYSANDRE.
FLAP FLAP FLAP
FLAP
GARDEVOIR, WE HAVE TO GO AFTER HER!
RMMRMMMBL
FLAP
TIERNO!
SHAUNA!
TRR

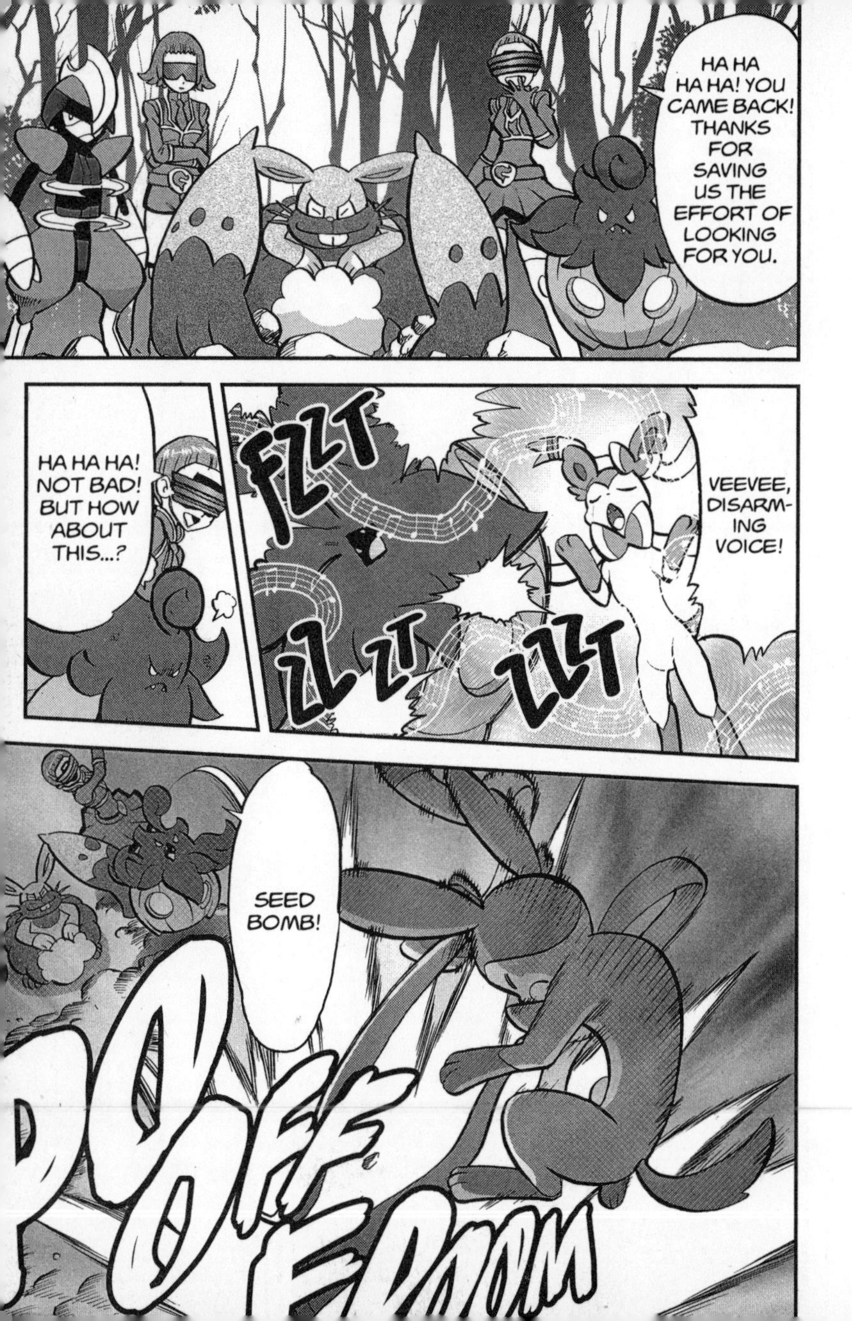
HA HA HA HA! YOU CAME BACK! THANKS FOR SAVING US THE EFFORT OF LOOKING FOR YOU.
VEEVEE, DISARMING VOICE!
FZZT
ZZZT
ZZ ZT
HA HA HA! NOT BAD! BUT HOW ABOUT THIS...?
SEED BOMB!

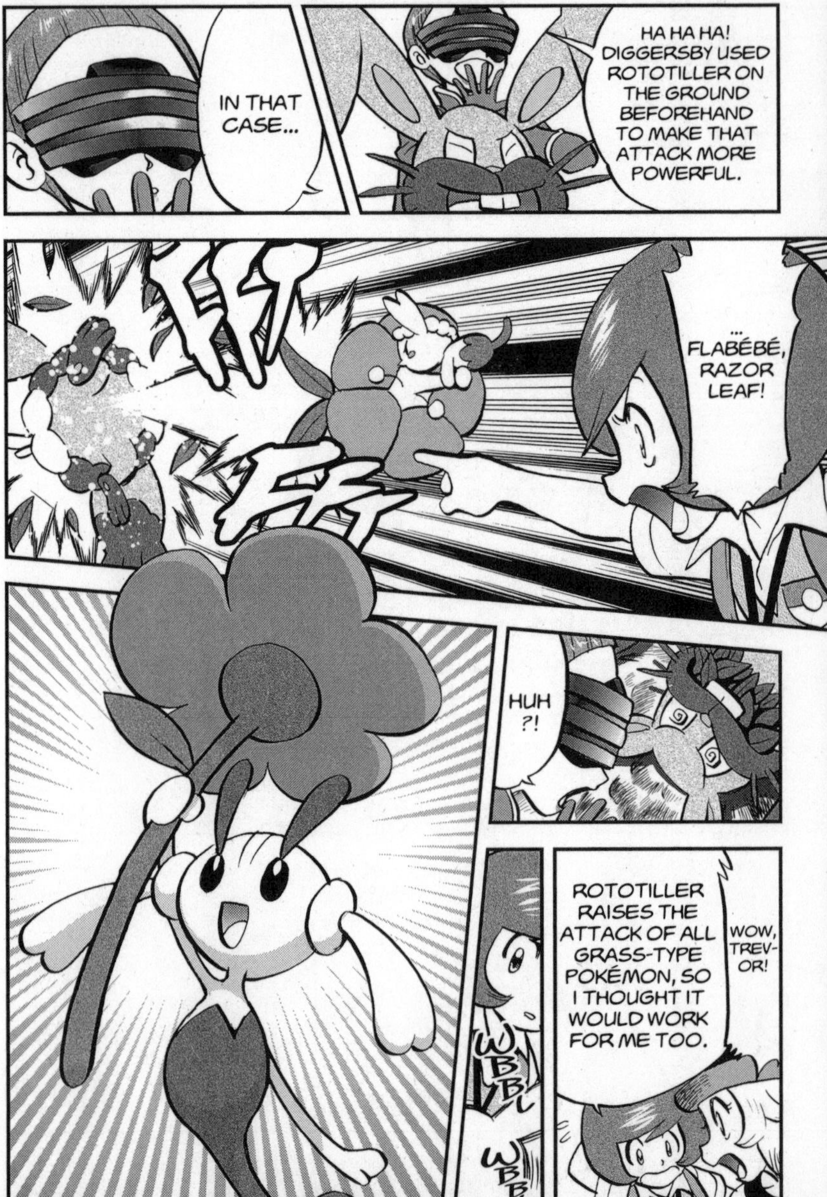
HA HA HA! DIGGERSBY USED ROTOTILLER ON THE GROUND BEFOREHAND TO MAKE THAT ATTACK MORE POWERFUL.
IN THAT CASE...
... FLABÉBÉ, RAZOR LEAF!
HUH ?!
ROTOTILLER RAISES THE ATTACK OF ALL GRASS-TYPE POKÉMON, SO I THOUGHT IT WOULD WORK FOR ME TOO.
WOW, TREV-OR!
WBBL
WBBL

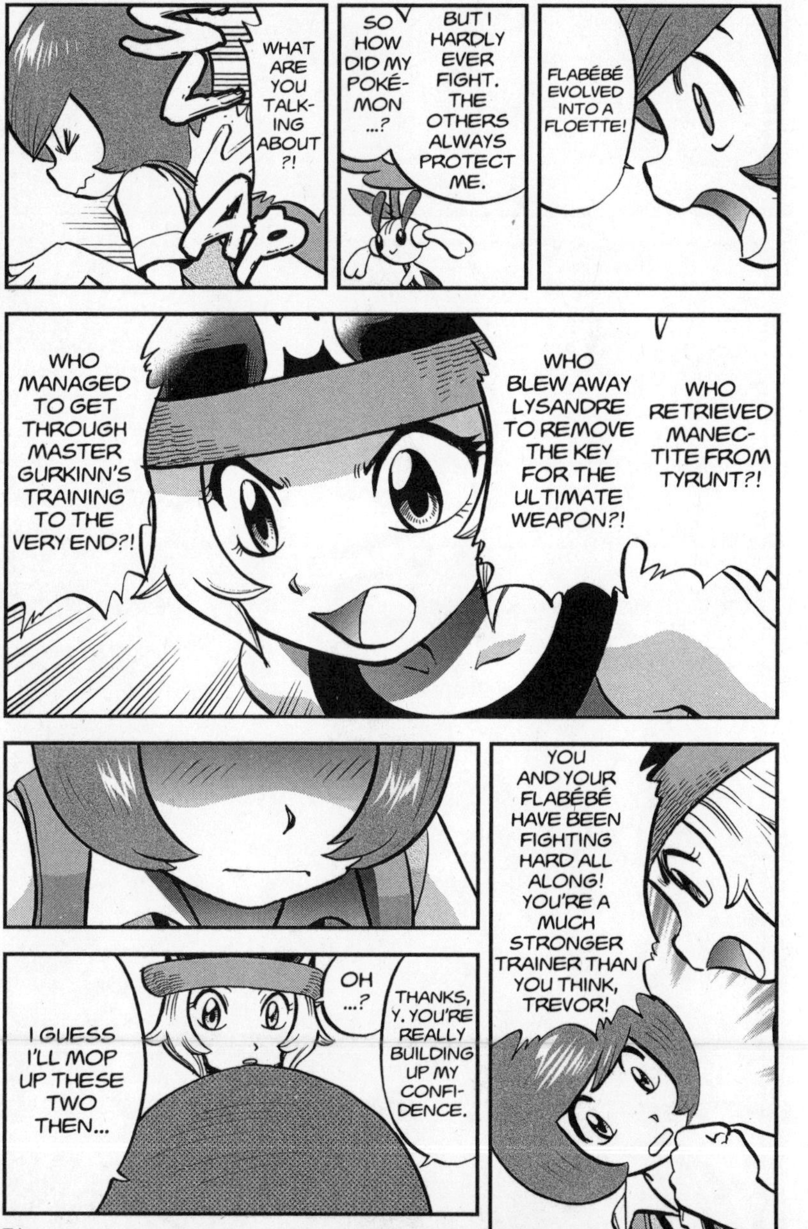
FLABÉBÉ EVOLVED INTO A FLOETTE!
BUT I HARDLY EVER FIGHT. THE OTHERS ALWAYS PROTECT ME.
SO HOW DID MY POKÉMON ...?
WHAT ARE YOU TALKING ABOUT ?!
WHO RETRIEVED MANECTITE FROM TYRUNT?!
WHO BLEW AWAY LYSANDRE TO REMOVE THE KEY FOR THE ULTIMATE WEAPON?!
WHO MANAGED TO GET THROUGH MASTER GURKINN'S TRAINING TO THE VERY END?!
YOU AND YOUR FLABÉBÉ HAVE BEEN FIGHTING HARD ALL ALONG! YOU'RE A MUCH STRONGER TRAINER THAN YOU THINK, TREVOR!
THANKS, Y. YOU'RE REALLY BUILDING UP MY CONFIDENCE.
OH ...?
I GUESS I'LL MOP UP THESE TWO THEN...

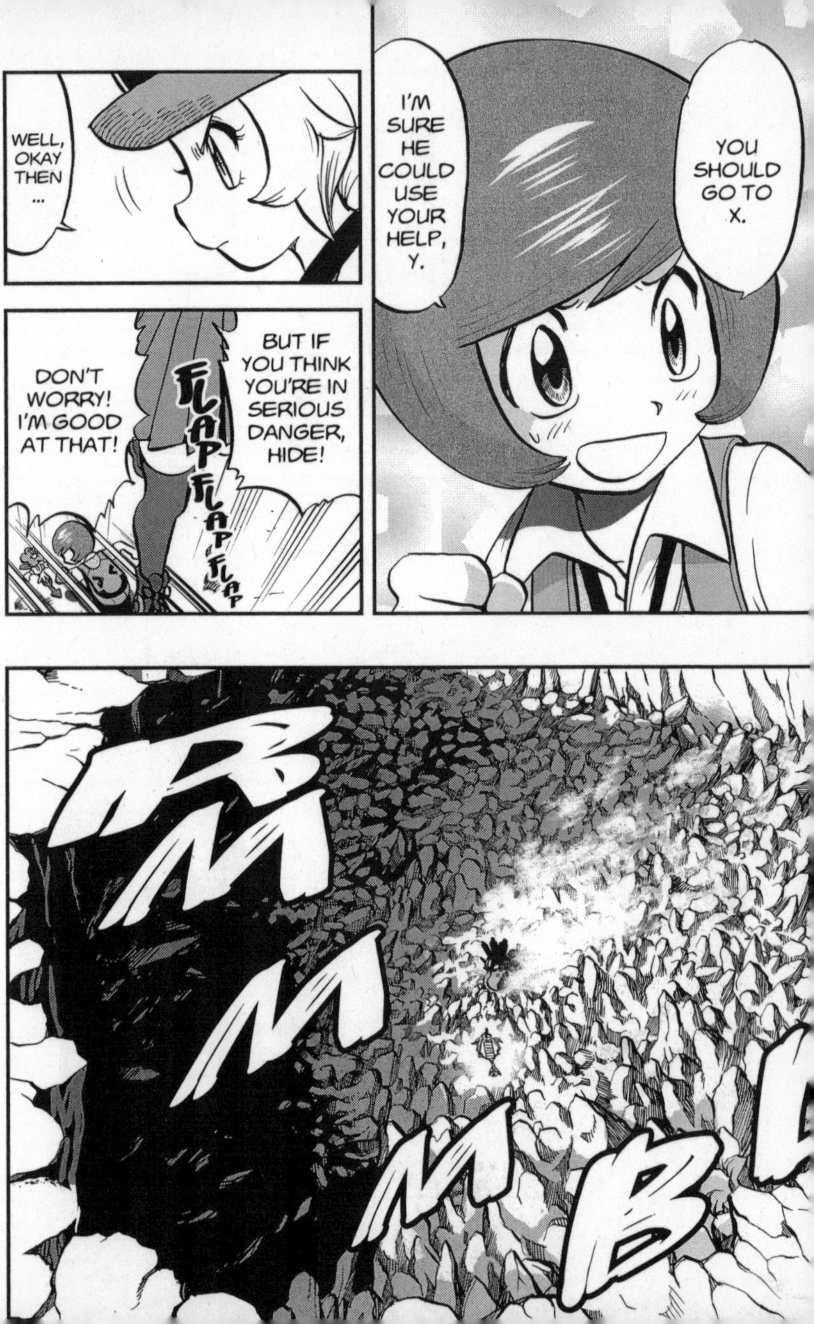
YOU SHOULD GO TO X.
I'M SURE HE COULD USE YOUR HELP, Y.
WELL, OKAY THEN ...
BUT IF YOU THINK YOU'RE IN SERIOUS DANGER, HIDE!
DON'T WORRY! I'M GOOD AT THAT!
FLAP FLAP FLAP FLAP
RMMMMB

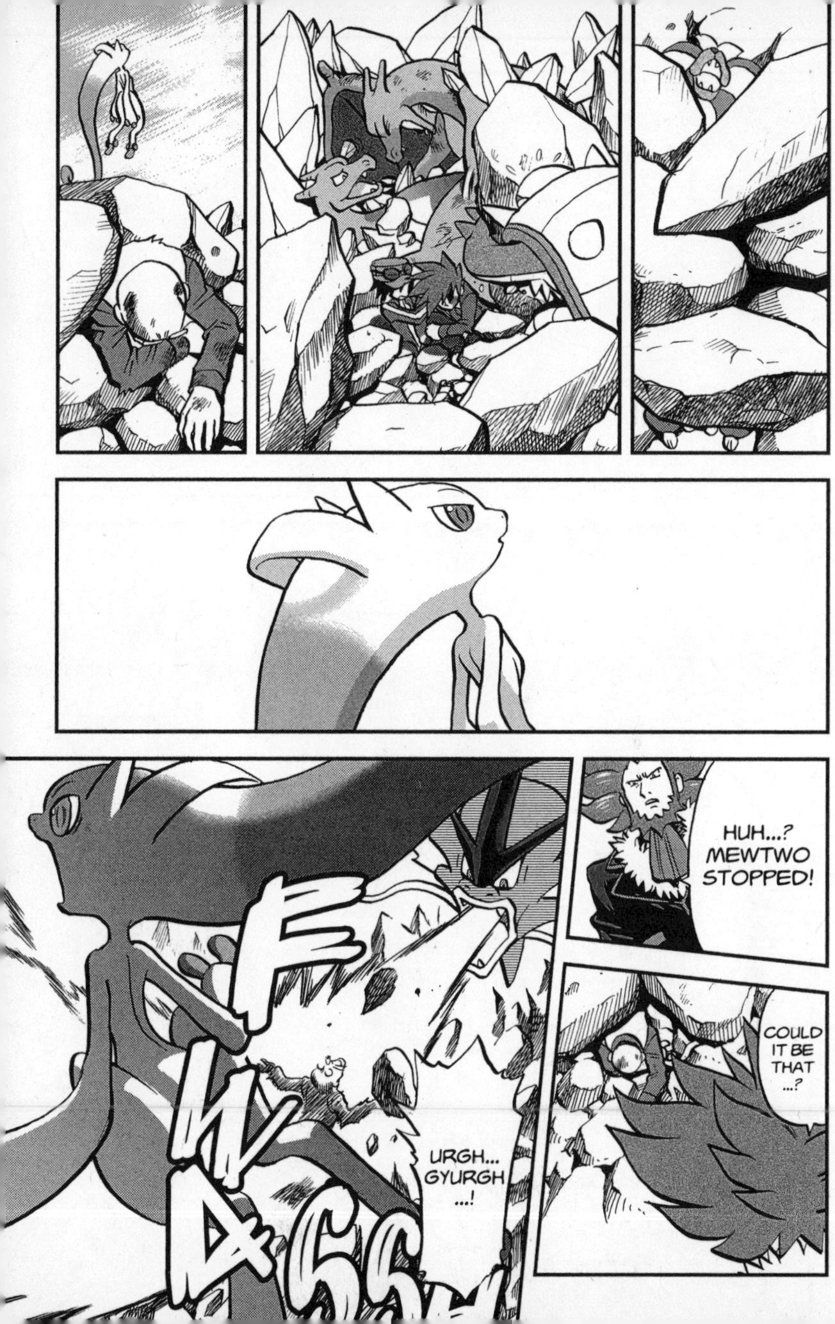
HUH...? MEWTWO STOPPED!
COULD IT BE THAT ...?
URGH... GYURGH ...!

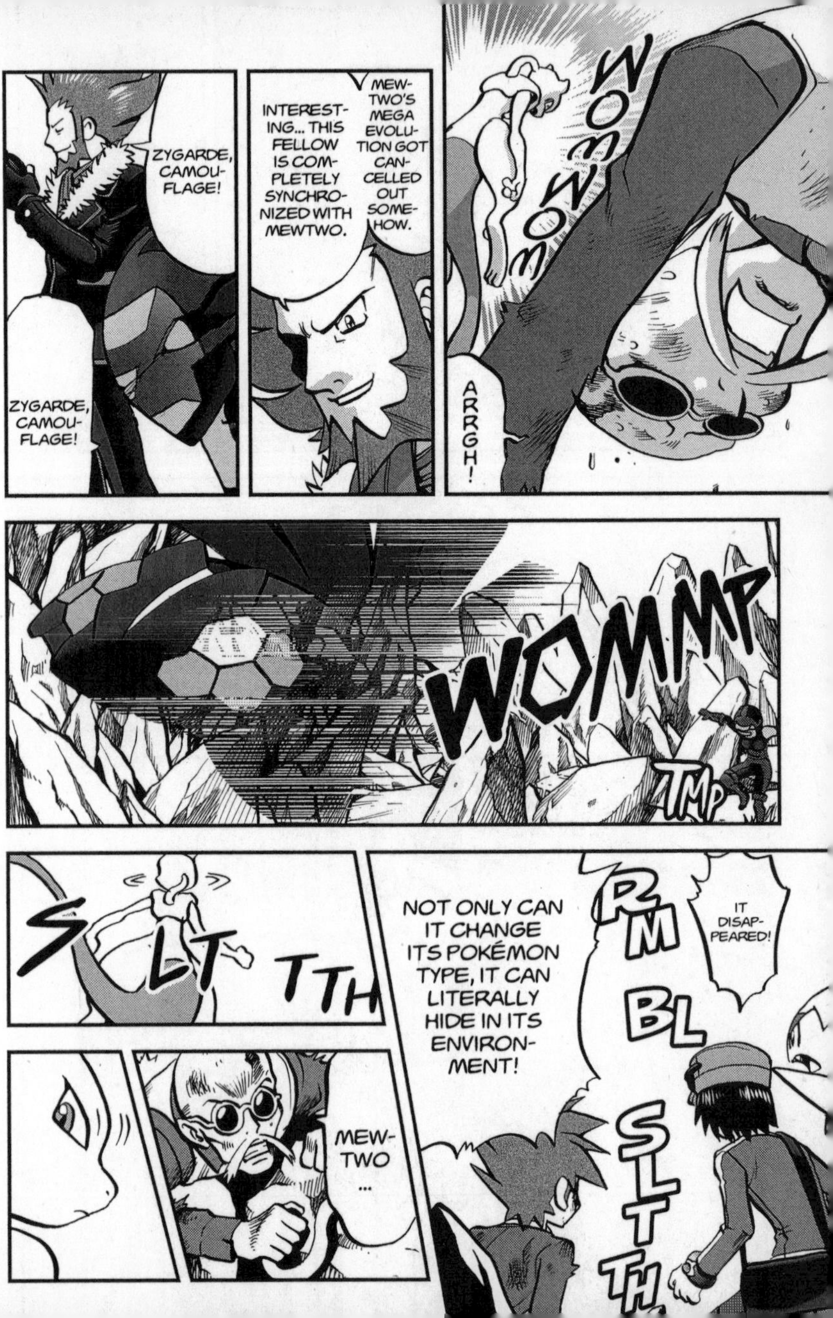
WOMWOMWOM
ARRGH!
MEW-TWO'S MEGA EVOLUTION GOT CANCELLED OUT SOMEHOW.
INTERESTING... THIS FELLOW IS COMPLETELY SYNCHRONIZED WITH MEWTWO.
ZYGARDE, CAMOUFLAGE!
ZYGARDE, CAMOUFLAGE!
WOMMP
TMP
IT DISAPPEARED!
RM BL
SLTTH
NOT ONLY CAN IT CHANGE ITS POKÉMON TYPE, IT CAN LITERALLY HIDE IN ITS ENVIRONMENT!
SLT TTH
MEW-TWO ...

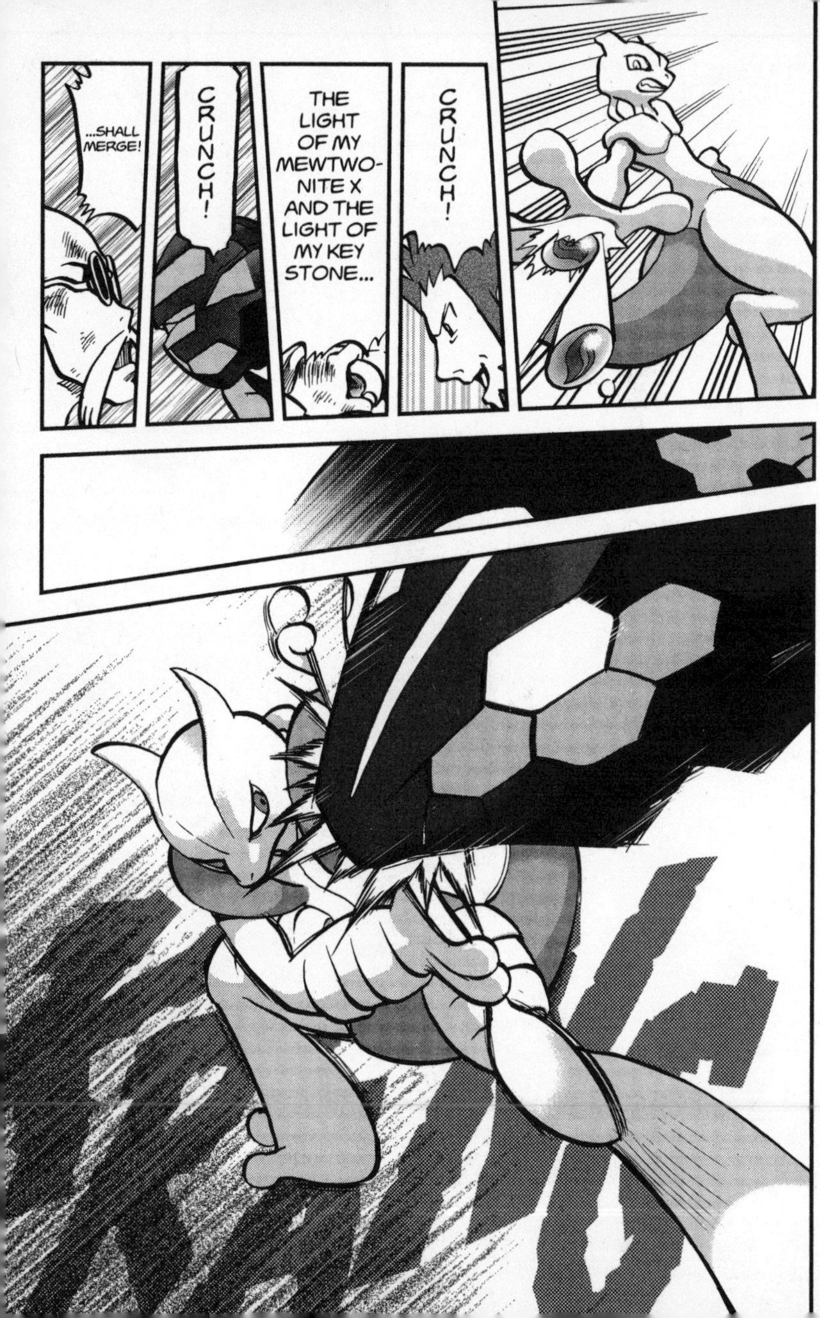
CRUNCH!
THE LIGHT OF MY MEWTWO-NITE X AND THE LIGHT OF MY KEY STONE...
CRUNCH!
...SHALL MERGE!

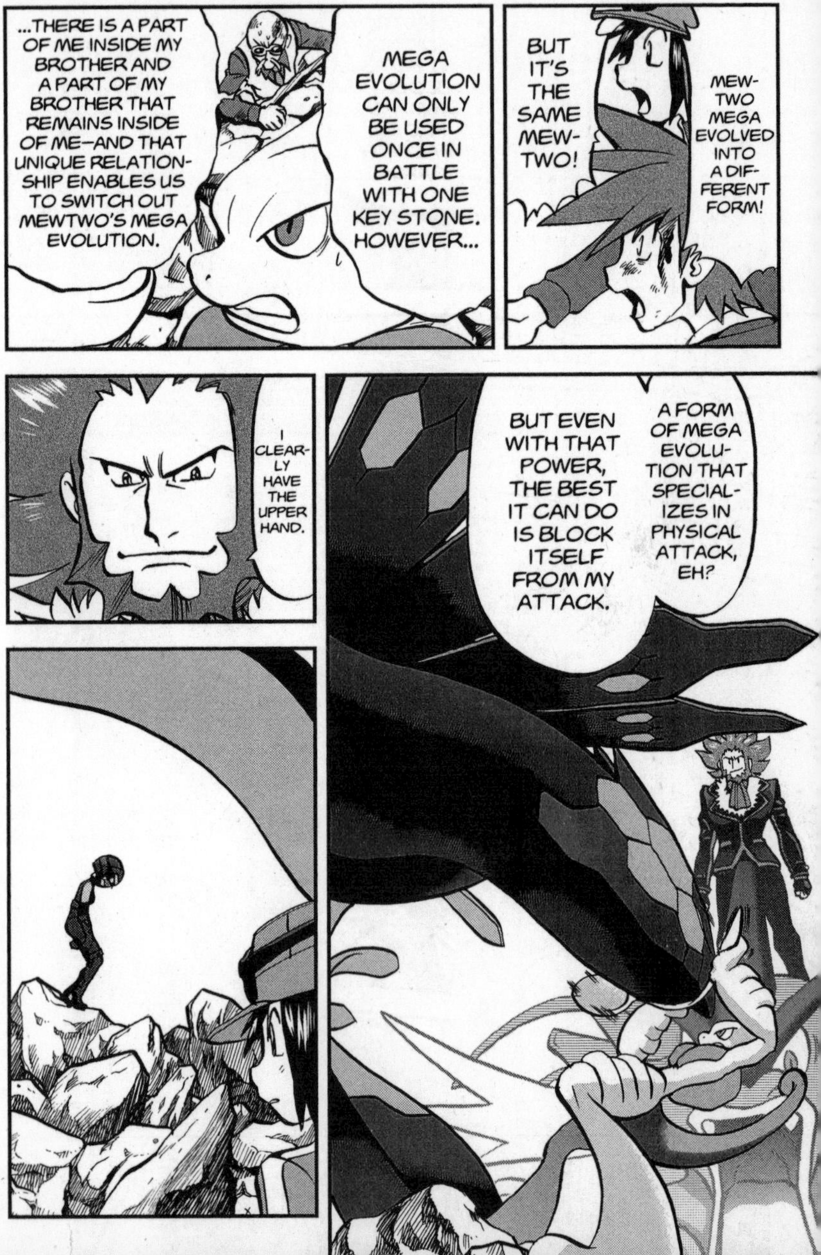
MEW-TWO MEGA EVOLVED INTO A DIF-FERENT FORM!
BUT IT'S THE SAME MEW-TWO!
MEGA EVOLUTION CAN ONLY BE USED ONCE IN BATTLE WITH ONE KEY STONE. HOWEVER...
...THERE IS A PART OF ME INSIDE MY BROTHER AND A PART OF MY BROTHER THAT REMAINS INSIDE OF ME--AND THAT UNIQUE RELATION-SHIP ENABLES US TO SWITCH OUT MEWTWO'S MEGA EVOLUTION.
A FORM OF MEGA EVOLU-TION THAT SPECIAL-IZES IN PHYSICAL ATTACK, EH?
BUT EVEN WITH THAT POWER, THE BEST IT CAN DO IS BLOCK ITSELF FROM MY ATTACK.
I CLEAR-LY HAVE THE UPPER HAND.

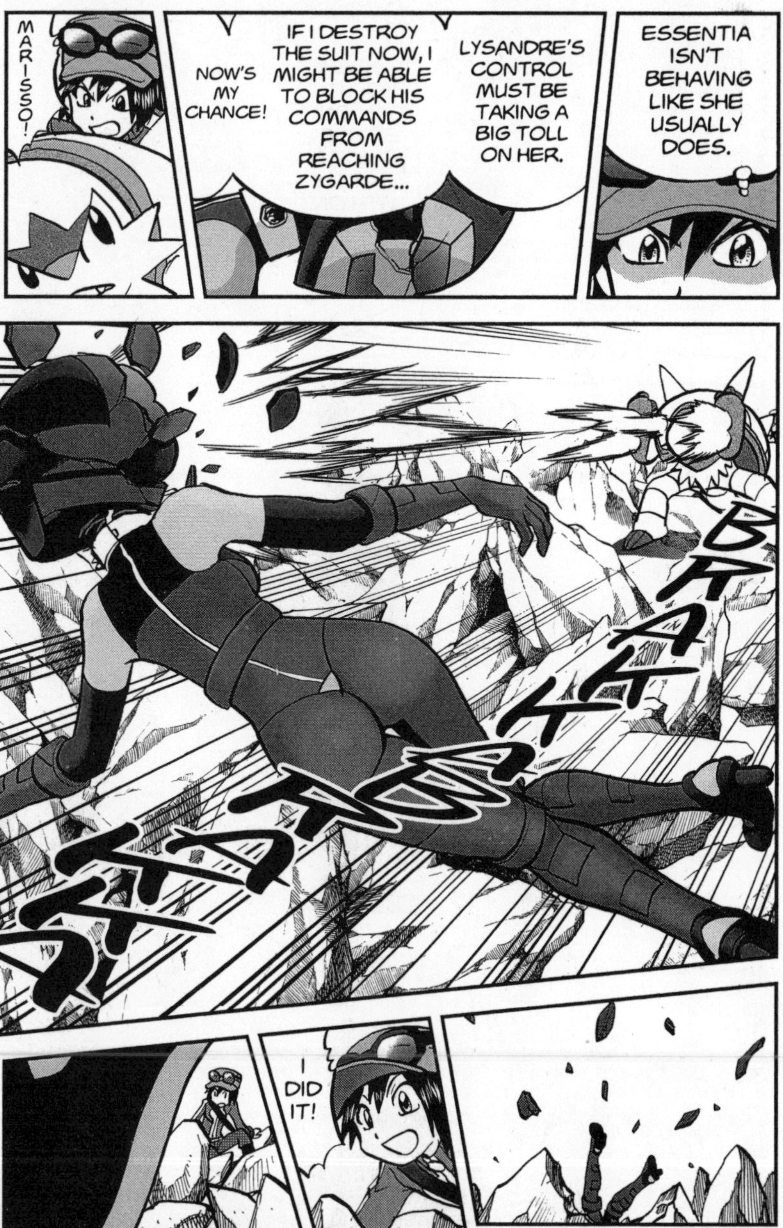
ESSENTIA ISN'T BEHAVING LIKE SHE USUALLY DOES.
LYSANDRE'S CONTROL MUST BE TAKING A BIG TOLL ON HER.
IF I DESTROY THE SUIT NOW, I MIGHT BE ABLE TO BLOCK HIS COMMANDS FROM REACHING ZYGARDE...
NOW'S MY CHANCE!
MARISSO!
I DID IT!

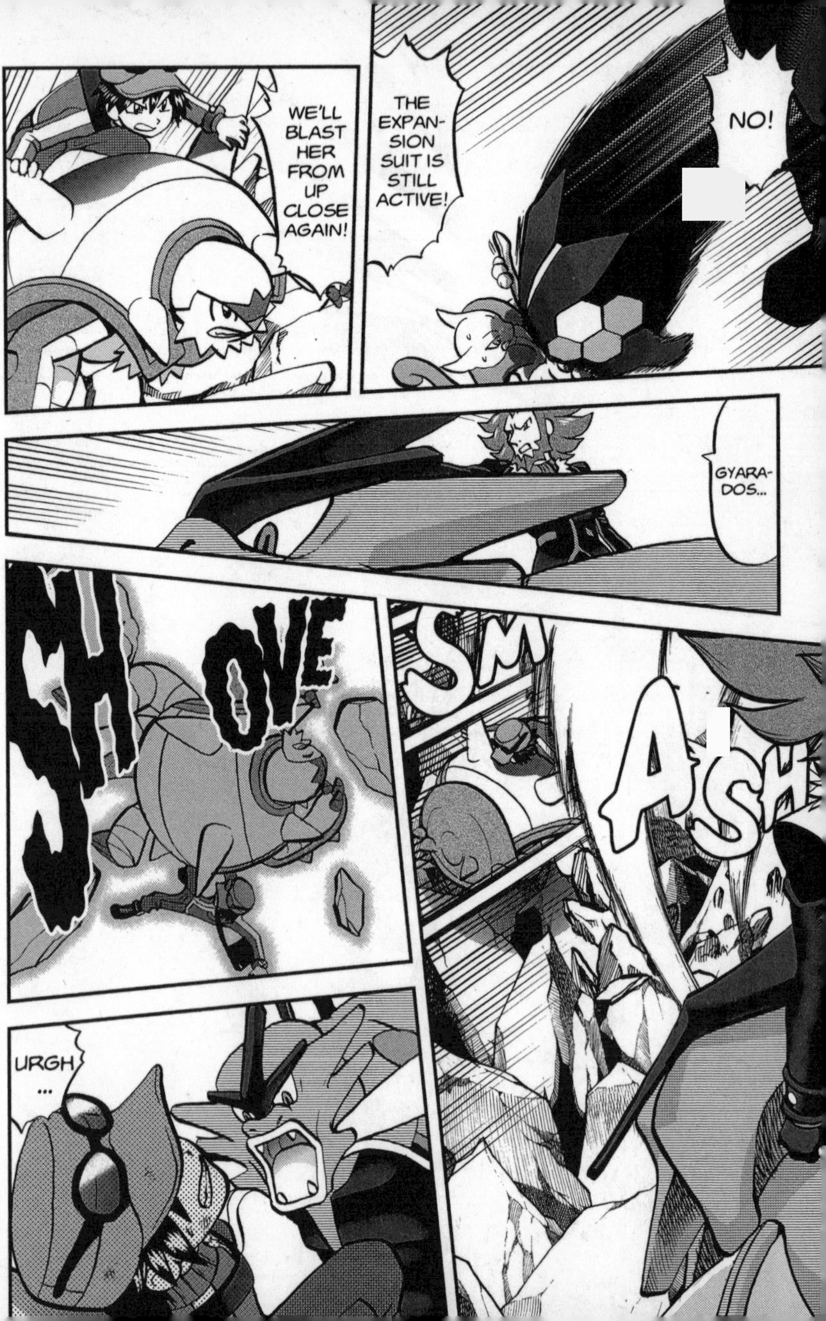
NO!
THE EXPANSION SUIT IS STILL ACTIVE!
WE'LL BLAST HER FROM UP CLOSE AGAIN!
GYARADOS...
SMASH
SHOVE
URGH...

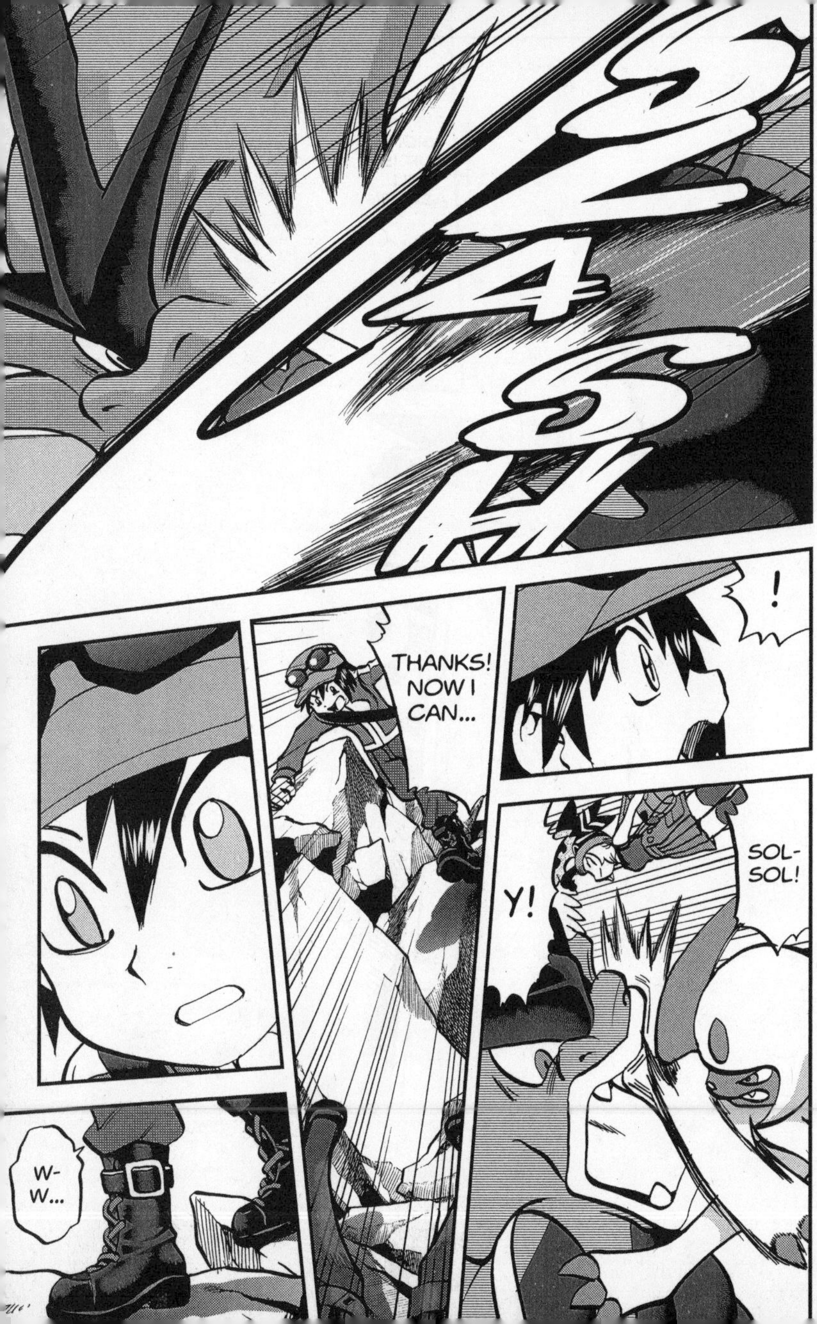
SLASH
!
SOL-SOL!
Y!
THANKS! NOW I CAN...
W-W...

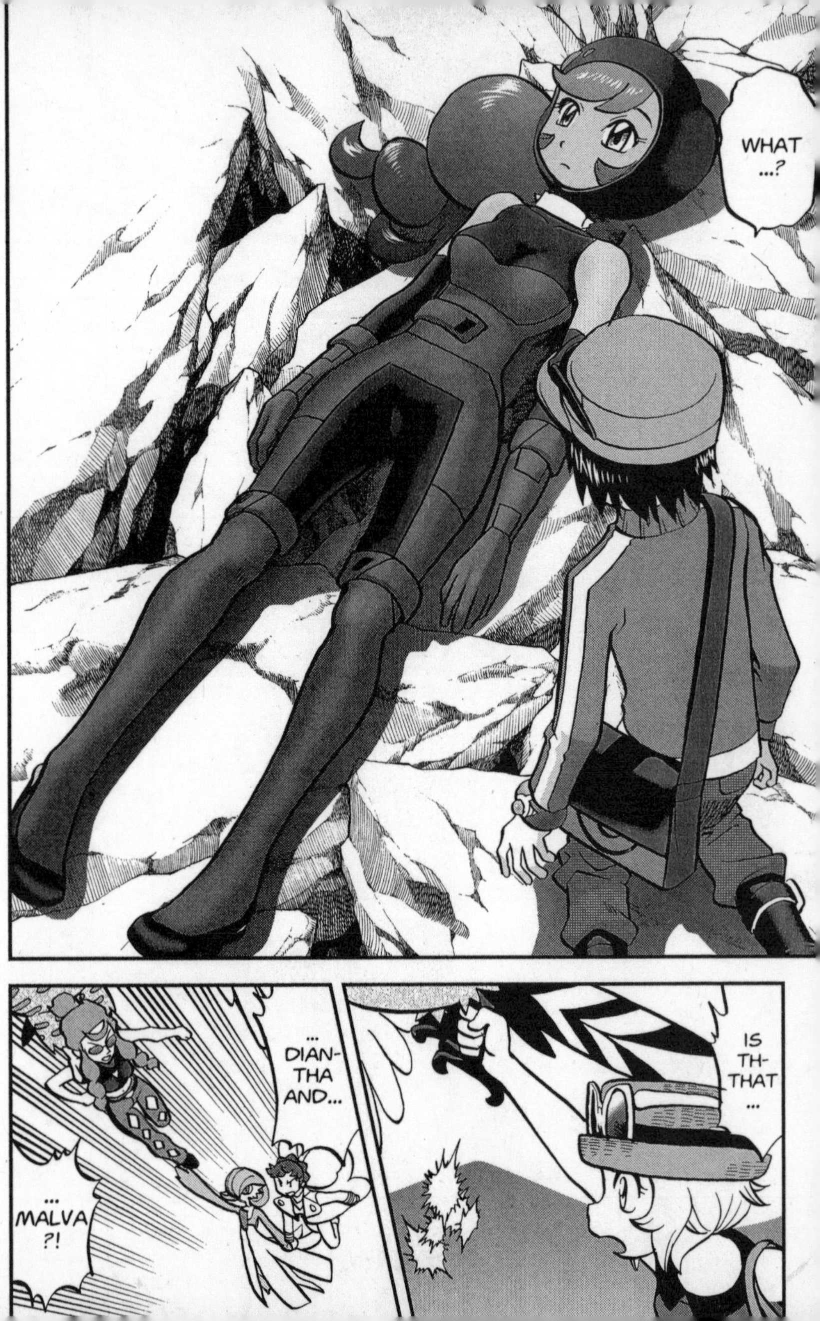
WHAT ...?
IS TH-THAT ...
... DIAN-THA AND...
... MALVA ?!

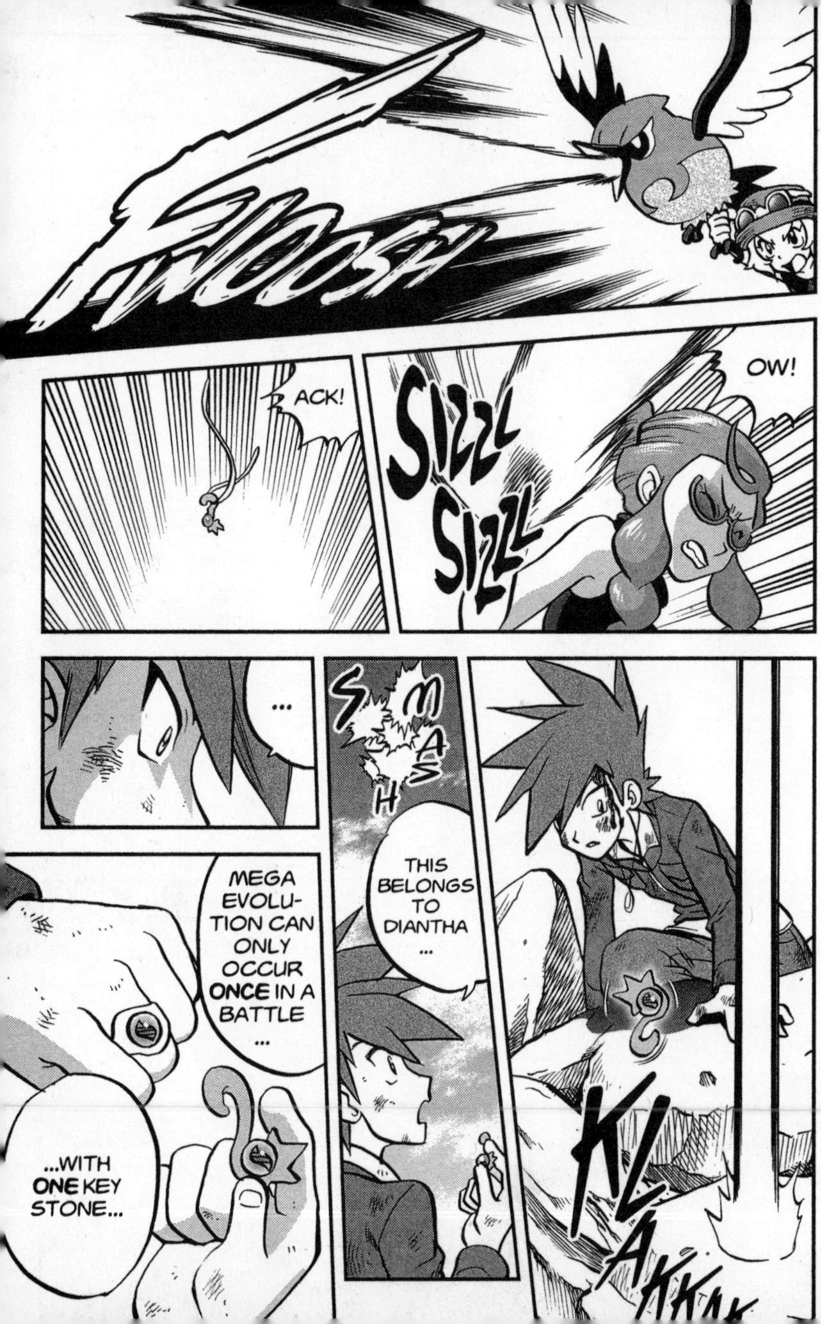
WHOOSH
OW!
SIZZL
SIZZL
ACK!
KLAKKAK
SMASH
THIS BELONGS TO DIANTHA ...
...
MEGA EVOLUTION CAN ONLY OCCUR ONCE IN A BATTLE ...
...WITH ONE KEY STONE...

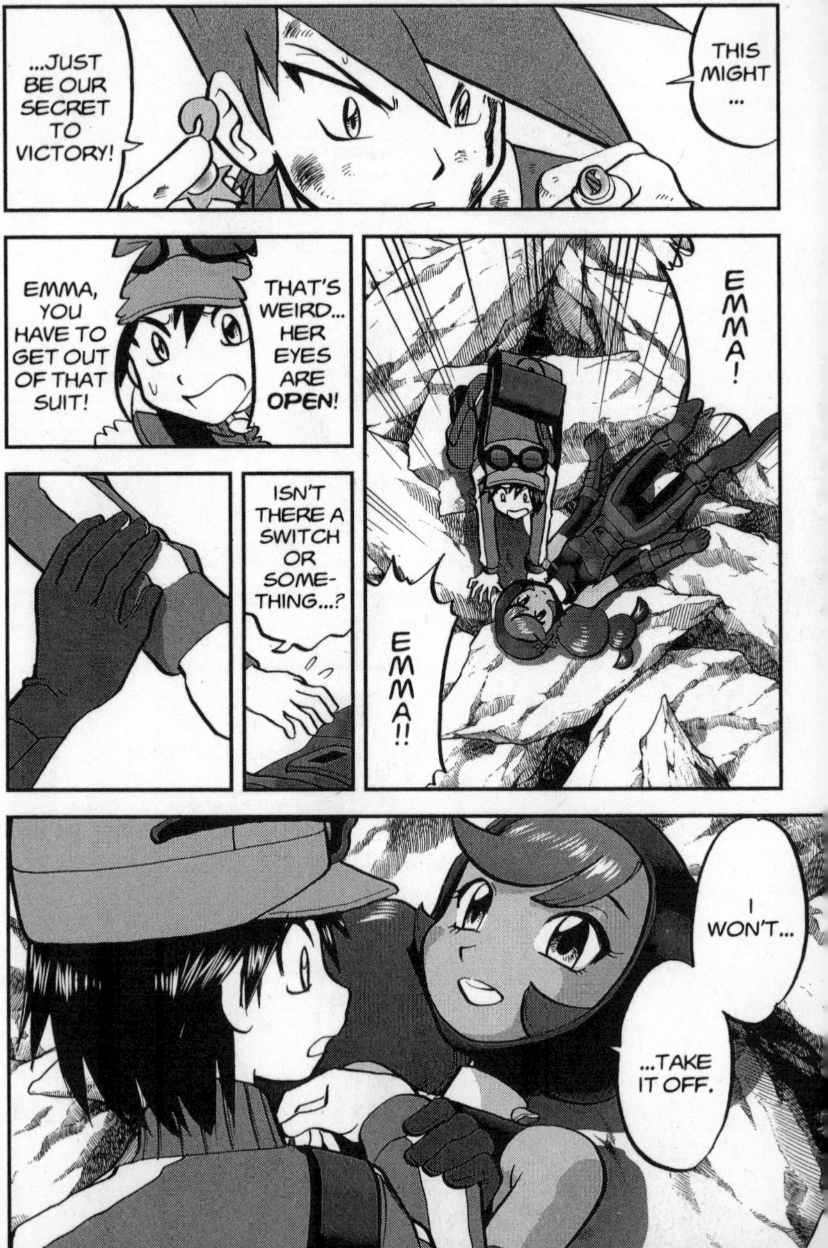
THIS MIGHT ...
...JUST BE OUR SECRET TO VICTORY!
EMMA!
EMMA!!
THAT'S WEIRD... HER EYES ARE **OPEN**!
EMMA, YOU HAVE TO GET OUT OF THAT SUIT!
ISN'T THERE A SWITCH OR SOME-THING...?
I WON'T...
...TAKE IT OFF.

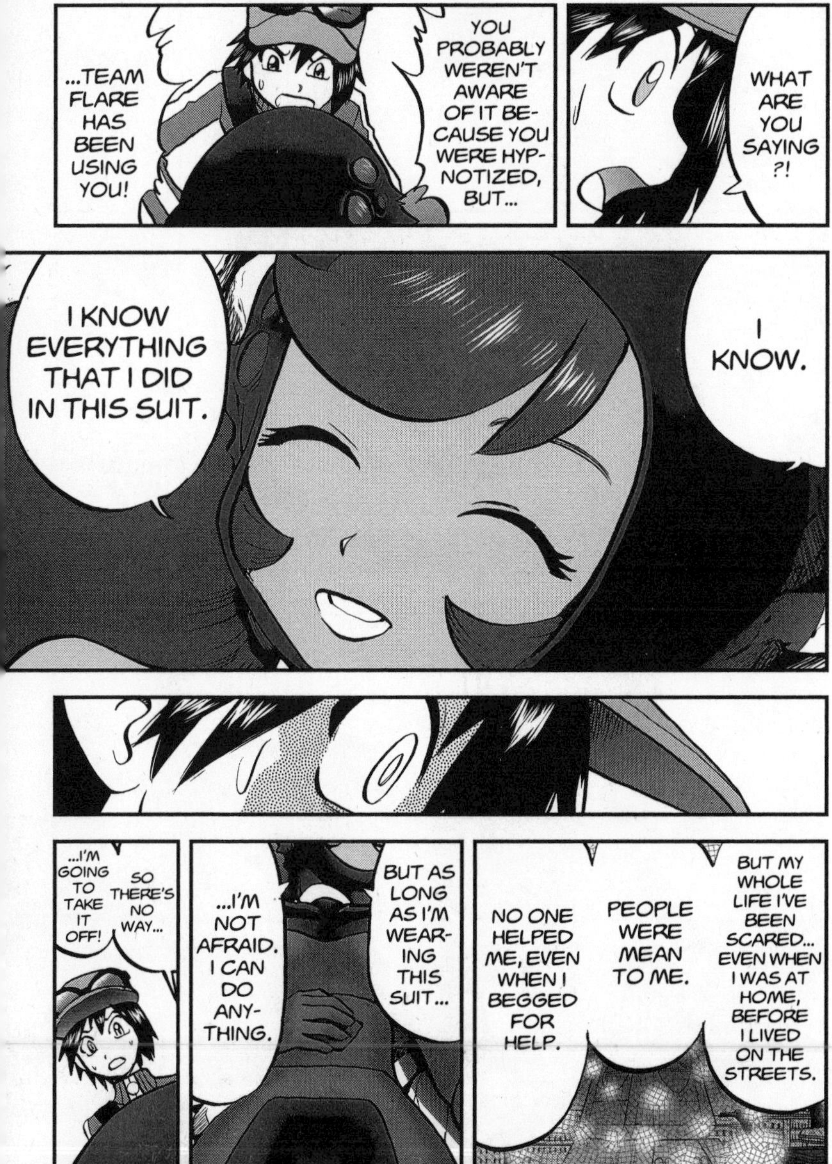
WHAT ARE YOU SAYING ?!
YOU PROBABLY WEREN'T AWARE OF IT BECAUSE YOU WERE HYPNOTIZED, BUT...
...TEAM FLARE HAS BEEN USING YOU!
I KNOW.
I KNOW EVERYTHING THAT I DID IN THIS SUIT.
BUT MY WHOLE LIFE I'VE BEEN SCARED... EVEN WHEN I WAS AT HOME, BEFORE I LIVED ON THE STREETS.
PEOPLE WERE MEAN TO ME.
NO ONE HELPED ME, EVEN WHEN I BEGGED FOR HELP.
BUT AS LONG AS I'M WEARING THIS SUIT...
...I'M NOT AFRAID. I CAN DO ANYTHING.
SO THERE'S NO WAY...
...I'M GOING TO TAKE IT OFF!

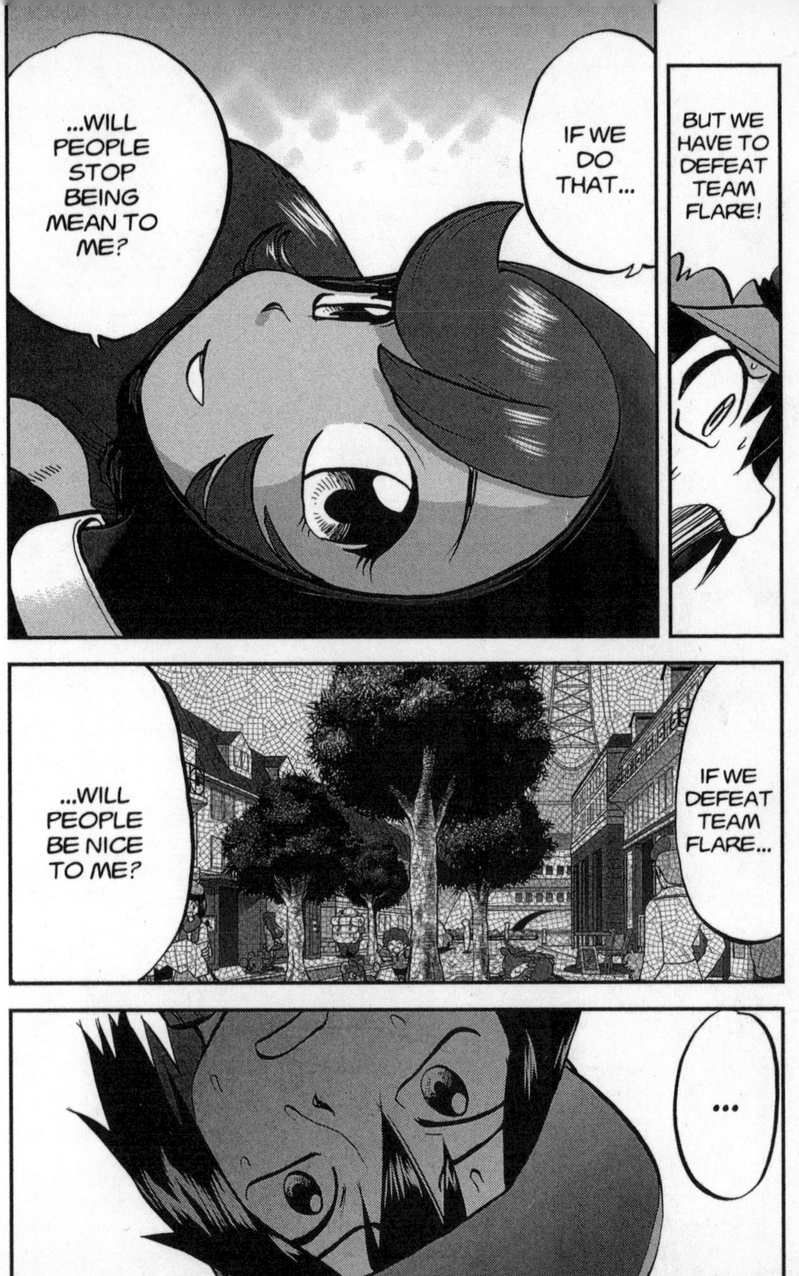
BUT WE HAVE TO DEFEAT TEAM FLARE!
IF WE DO THAT...
...WILL PEOPLE STOP BEING MEAN TO ME?
IF WE DEFEAT TEAM FLARE...
...WILL PEOPLE BE NICE TO ME?
...

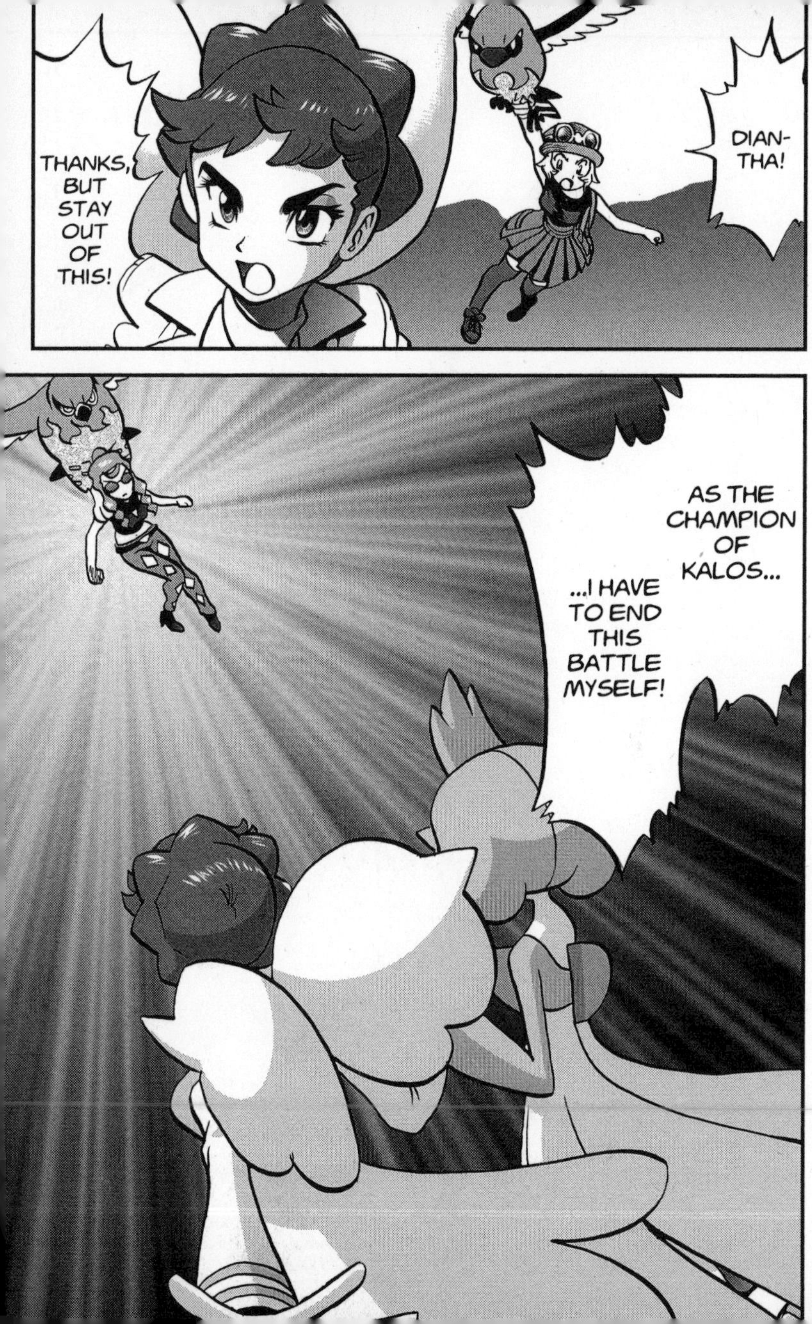
DIAN-THA!
THANKS, BUT STAY OUT OF THIS!
AS THE CHAMPION OF KALOS...
...I HAVE TO END THIS BATTLE MYSELF!

Pokémon Village

Legends say a place exists where
Pokémon live in hiding, but no
one has ever found it.

Pokémon X • Y
Volume 11
Perfect Square Edition

Story by HIDENORI KUSAKA
Art by SATOSHI YAMAMOTO

©2017 The Pokémon Company International.
©1995-2017 Nintendo/Creatures Inc./GAME FREAK inc.
TM, ®, and character names are trademarks of Nintendo.
POCKET MONSTERS SPECIAL X•Y Vol. 6
by Hidenori KUSAKA, Satoshi YAMAMOTO
© 2014 Hidenori KUSAKA, Satoshi YAMAMOTO
All rights reserved.
Original Japanese edition published by SHOGAKUKAN.
English translation rights in the United States of America, Canada, the United
Kingdom, Ireland, Australia, New Zealand and India arranged with SHOGAKUKAN.

English Adaptation—Bryant Turnage
Translation—Tetsuichiro Miyaki
Touch-up & Lettering—Annaliese Christman
Design—Alice Lewis
Editor—Annette Roman

Printed in the U.S.A.

Published by
VIZ Media, LLC
P.O. Box 77010
San Francisco, CA 94107

10 9 8 7 6 5 4 3 2 1
First printing, July 2017

www.perfectsquare.com   www.viz.com

PARENTAL ADVISORY
POKÉMON ADVENTURES
is rated A and is suitable
for readers of all ages.
RATED A FOR ALL AGES
ratings.viz.com

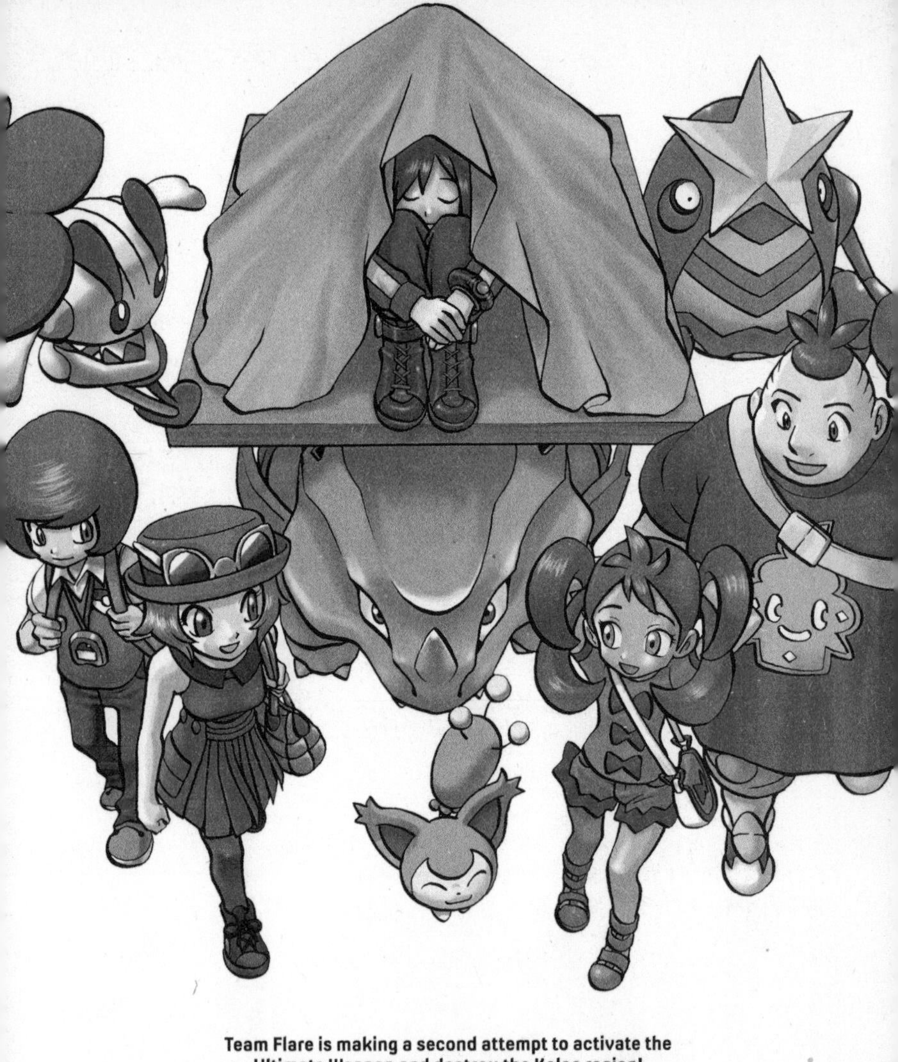

Team Flare is making a second attempt to activate the Ultimate Weapon and destroy the Kalos region! And this time, X, Y and friends will need some truly expert help to put a stop to their nefarious plan and heartless methods. Then our friends are faced with a moral dilemma...

Also, will Yveltal and Xerneas fight for eternity...?

VOLUME 12 AVAILABLE OCTOBER 2017!

FINAL VOLUME!

Begin your Pokémon Adventure here in the Kanto region!

POKÉMON™
ADVENTURES
RED & BLUE BOX SET

Story by **HIDENORI KUSAKA**   Art by **MATO**

Includes
**POKÉMON
ADVENTURES**
Vols. 1-7
and a collectible
poster!

**All your favorite Pokémon game
characters jump out of the screen into
the pages of this action-packed manga!**

Red doesn't just want to train Pokémon, he wants
to be their friend too. Bulbasaur and Poliwhirl seem game.
But independent Pikachu won't be so easy to win over!

And watch out for Team Rocket, Red...
They only want to be your enemy!

Start the adventure today!

Pokémon ADVENTURES

HEARTGOLD & SOULSILVER

by HIDENORI KUSAKA
y SATOSHI YAMAMOTO

In this **two-volume** thriller, troublemaker Gold and feisty Silver must team up again to find their old enemy Lance and the Legendary Pokémon Arceus!

Available now!

Pokémon™

POCKET COMICS

STORY & ART BY SANTA HARUKAZE

BLACK & WHITE
$9.99 US / $10.99 CAN

LEGENDARY POKÉMON
$9.99 US / $10.99 CAN

X•Y
$12.99 US / $13.99 CAN

A Pokémon pocket-sized book chock-full of four-panel gags, Pokémon trivia and fun quizzes based on the characters you know and love!

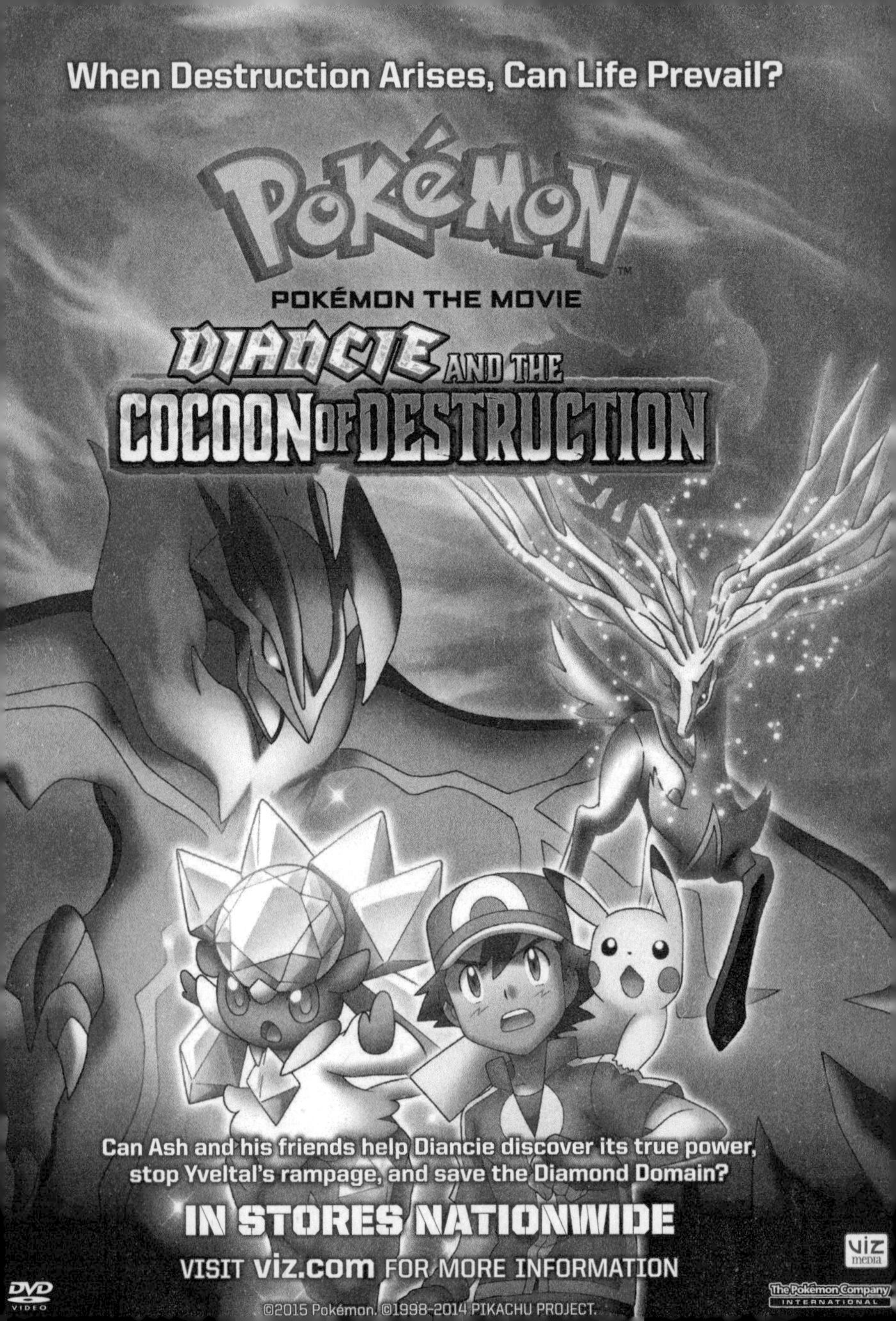
When Destruction Arises, Can Life Prevail?
POKéMON
POKÉMON THE MOVIE
DIANCIE AND THE COCOON OF DESTRUCTION
Can Ash and his friends help Diancie discover its true power, stop Yveltal's rampage, and save the Diamond Domain?
IN STORES NATIONWIDE
VISIT viz.com FOR MORE INFORMATION
DVD VIDEO
viz media
The Pokémon Company INTERNATIONAL
©2015 Pokémon. ©1998-2014 PIKACHU PROJECT.

A NEW MEGA ADVENTURE

THE SERIES XY

Ash Ketchum's journey continues in **Pokémon the Series: XY** as he arrives in the Kalos region, a land bursting with beauty, full of new Pokémon to be discovered!

24 ACTION-PACKED EPISODES!

Pick up **Pokémon the Series: XY** today!

IN STORES NATIONWIDE

visit **viz.com** for more information

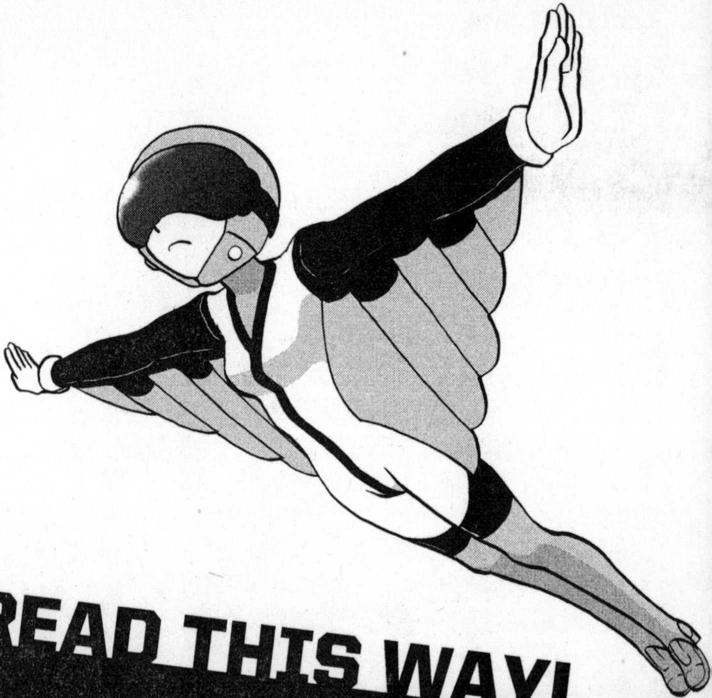

‹‹‹ READ THIS WAY!

THIS IS THE END OF THIS GRAPHIC NOVEL!

To properly enjoy this VIZ Media graphic novel, please turn it around and begin reading from right to left.

This book has been printed in the original Japanese format in order to preserve the orientation of the original artwork. Have fun with it!

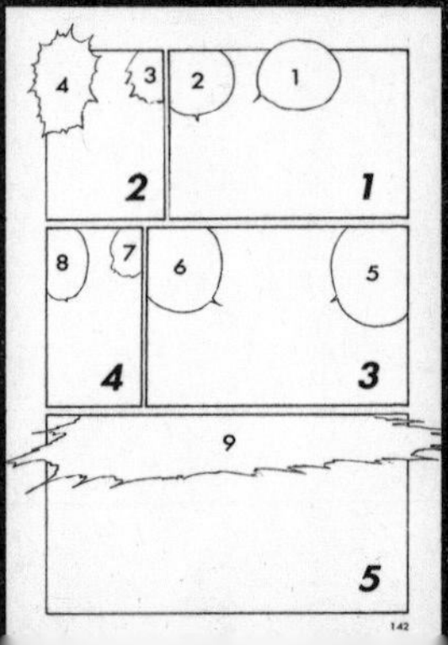
1
2
3
4
5
6
7
8
9
1
2
3
4
5
142